CALL THE KEEPER

CALL THE KEEPER

a novel by NAT HENTOFF

NEW YORK · THE VIKING PRESS

FOR MARGOT

CALL THE KEEPER

"The endless isolation of Man makes enmity impossible."

—BERTOLT BRECHT, *In the Jungle of the Cities*, 1923

"You are putting me on."

—JOHN THE AVENGER

1

Billy

Thomas was out on his feet. His feet were more or less making it, but the rest of him was somewhere else. It was about one in the morning, on Sixth Avenue, a block from where he lives on Christopher Street. He was a good, nonaggressive drunk, Thomas. First he'd get terribly quiet, then paralysis would set in, and then he'd go to sleep. He could have been asleep, walking, that night.

A few doors behind him was the rhinoceros—Harry Sanders, grisly proof that the black man can rise in this here open society. Sanders was a plainclothesman, but even a blind man could tell he was a cop. By his beat. The rhythm of his walk and his grunt. You can tell a lot about a guy from his natural time. And then, as soon as Sanders opened his mouth, you could hear the knee in the stomach in the squad room.

Seeing that cement mixer of a body trying to blend into the shadows, I knew Thomas had seen my sister some time that night. Sanders had very few principles that weren't negotiable, but one of them was no race mixing in bed. Or to be more accurate, black for black. Especially where my sister was concerned. Sanders snuffs around the building where Dianne and I share a place like he's our private police force.

Thomas lumbered ahead and I eased up to Sanders. "You gonna wait until he bumps into somebody and then bust him for assault?"

"Got no time for you, boy." Sanders' voice came from way down inside him—a thick gurgle.

"Been watching over Dianne?"

"You're some black brother, boy. Letting her make it with that—" He pointed his snout toward stumbling Thomas.

"Do I have to choose between him and you? Because if I do—" Sanders cracked me up the side of my head. I moved into the middle of the street. Makes no sense tangling with a cop. White cop, black cop, makes no sense.

"Because if I do," I got ready to run, "I'd rather she was a bull dike like your mother." Sanders ignored me and put his eyes back on Thomas.

Now I don't give a good goddamn about Thomas. Never have, all the years I've been working with him at the radio station. I don't like him and I don't dislike him. He's just there. But being bugged at Sanders, I decided to tag along in case I might find out something I could use later. When he got to his apartment building, Thomas almost walked through the doorman. I watched him go up in the elevator and Sanders go up the street toward Sheridan Square. Sooner or later Sanders would get him, but I didn't figure it would be that night.

2

Dianne

I had seen Thomas that night, but not for long. He was wrestling with his motivations again, and it was a drag.

"Dianne, am I in love with you because you're Negro or in spite of it? Or is it a mixture of both—and more?"

"Baby, why don't you schedule a panel discussion about it on that damn radio station of yours? Only leave me OUT of it." And I walked out of the bar. He tried to follow me, but his engine room was already flooded so I had no trouble shaking him.

Just outside the door, there was Sanders. He tried to look surprised, as if I were the last person he expected to see right there that minute.

"Detective Sanders, to whom do I complain about a man who keeps bothering me all the time?"

He grinned like a bulldog about to get a bone with a lot of meat on it.

"At your service, Miss Burnett."

"Well, tell yourself to get lost. Stop using the taxpayers' time to protect my virtue. I'm a big girl."

He put a hand on my sleeve. Gently. As gentle as he could be. It hurt.

"Off!"

He stuck it in his pocket. "A drink?" he rumbled. "Could I buy you a drink?"

"Detective Sanders, I don't dig you. Any which way. Please cease obstructing one of your employers." And I left him standing there looking as if he were about to howl to the moon.

Since I was so close to St. Mark's Place, I went to see Shirley. She had the baby in one arm and a copy of *The Autobiography of Malcolm X* in the other.

"Where's the Avenger?"

"Out whipping the white folks. Some symposium at the Five Spot."

"He still hiding you?"

"He'd like to. If only I were just a shade darker, I could pass. It's ridiculous. All the interviews with him mention he's got a white wife. And all his nationalist buddies know it. But still, he insists on going to those hate baths without me. He says I make him uncomfortable, and I bet I do."

Shirley seemed thinner every time I saw her. She was only about five feet to start with, and that night she looked like any sudden movement would make a bone pop through her skin. With her big black eyes and shaggy black hair and the way she was drawn so tightly into herself, she looked like a Jew child that had just been liberated from Auschwitz. But fragile she wasn't.

We had some beer and I was doing an imitation of Thomas playing tag with his identities—to use his favorite word—when the Avenger came home. John is as thin as Shirley but almost a foot and a half taller. And he carries himself so straight that, with his tight lips and hollow eyes, he comes into a room like the black angel of death, come down—or up, depending on your eschatology—to collect all the due bills. Right now.

The Avenger nodded at me, nodded at Shirley, looked into the crib where the baby was whanging away at a Busy Box, grabbed a can of beer from the refrigerator, and sat down on the edge of a chair. It was all done in one continuous motion, and, as an obbligato, John was humming a new tune by Grachan Moncur. It was off his last LP.

"What was the message tonight?" Shirley asked.

"Blood," John grinned. "Blood in the streets."

"When are you going to get tired of that crap?" Shirley stroked his head.

"It's not crap, baby. That's what's going to happen."

"And then what?"

"It'll go on a long time once it starts. Things can change during that long time."

"A holding action, John?" I poured myself some more beer. "Until our black and yellow brothers from all over the world come to rescue us?"

"Maybe, baby."

"Well," Shirley put a hand on her heart, threw her head back, and hollered, "it's too late for me, but maybe my baby will make it."

I giggled. John smiled too, but hard. "I hope that color he is will be black enough."

"Jesus Christ!" Shirley banged the table. "Why don't you put on some cowboy boots and buy a big cap pistol so you can do all this in costume?"

John got up, went into the bedroom, and came back with a small, black pistol.

"Get that fucking thing OUT of here!" Shirley yelled. "How long have you had that?"

"A couple of days." John fondled the gun. "You never know when a time will come. Got to be ready. Now, suppose some cop busts in here, like they do, and pushes you and the baby around. You think I'm going to take that?"

"Yes," said Shirley.

"You don't know nothing, Shirley. You don't know a damn thing about me."

"Oh cut it out," she said, calmed down. "You got a lousy audience for your act."

"I sure as hell have." He got up and moved toward the door.

"Listen," Shirley said, her voice rising again, "you come back without that gun!"

John smiled like a wolf. "You got nothing to be afraid of."

"I know that, you idiot. I'm worried about you."

"Us natives will get along, ma'am."

"Damn it!" She bit her lip, grabbed *The Autobiography of Malcolm X,* and threw it at him. John stepped aside, and the book hit the door. "See? Black magic. That book wouldn't hurt me." He tossed the book back at her, bowed slightly to me, and left.

Shirley leaned back and swallowed hard. "You better leave, Dianne, I'm going to cry. Just for myself, for once."

"One thing, Shirley. If that pig Sanders comes by, you don't know where I went except I said I wasn't coming back. I don't want him stalking this place—with John in that kind of mood."

"Yeah," Shirley muttered. "Damn. How did a nice Jewish girl get mixed up in all this?"

"You were lucky, Shirley. Think how much more interesting it is than marrying a dentist in Queens."

"Or than having leukemia. See you."

On the street I looked around, but no Sanders. I bet he's tailing Thomas, I thought. Poor Thomas. Poor Shirley. Poor John. Maybe even poor Sanders. But I'm not a social worker so I bought a fifth of J & B, picked up the *Times,* and walked home. I was through with *that* night.

3

Thomas

A blackout. A real, honest-to-God void. Not a metaphor, but the actual horror of not knowing what I did—or said. I remember three bars after Dianne left, and the next thing I remember is lying here on my bed. I was getting sick because the room was turning and I just couldn't get up to steady it. I couldn't even get up far enough to fall back. I guess that's what certain kinds of strokes are like. Only intelligence is left. And feeling. And desperation. Then the banging started. Somebody was pounding, pounding at the door as if he had a hammer. A sledgehammer. I needed to get up and answer. I had to. It was terribly important I open the door. I don't know why, but it was. All I could do was keep croaking, "Who is it? Who is it? Coming. Coming." The banging got worse. And I kept trying to get up. That's all I remember.

4

Randal

Thomas was to have come by that night, but he never showed. We were going to talk about a new program I'd do for the radio station. Something like "Jazz from the Inside." You know, how a musician hears what's happening. New records, old records, interviews with guys on the scene and jazz players out of the past. Music wasn't Thomas's bag at the station, but he figured he could talk the program director into the idea. But I wasn't that sure. The program director was Negro, and here am I—maybe the blondest WASP in all of jazz. Jazz from the *inside*?

Anyway, came two in the morning and no Thomas. And no customers. Well, there were two cats strung out in a booth. And the press agent for the club. Mr. Hippie. We were supposed to hit for the last set, but Mason looked at me and shook his head. He opened his case, put his tenor in, and went into the men's room.

Behind the bar, Steve, one of the owners, shook *his* head. "He could have asked."

"What was to ask?" I said. "You expect a line in ten minutes? It's the middle of the week, man." I'd put my guitar away and was waiting for Steve to offer a drink.

"Bourbon?" Steve poured without waiting for an answer. "You going to stay with Mason?" He jerked his head toward the men's room.

"If he wants," I said. "He's an easy guy to work for. Personally, I mean. The music's something else. You can't cool it with him. Some nights he'll pull something in the middle of a tune and I feel like I've just stepped into an empty elevator shaft. But that's good. Keeps me from getting comfortable."

"Does it ever bug you," Mr. Hippie slithered over, "being the only white guy in that combo?"

"I don't feel a draft from them. Does it bother *you?*"

Mason was back. His size—six three—made Mr. Hippie have to look up at him, and that he didn't like. Especially since Mason looked down at him as if he ought to step on him. "Since when you counting by color?" Mason said coldly.

"*You* always do," said Mr. Hippie. "I mean you're always saying the blacker you are, the more jazz you can play."

Mason was so black they still hadn't figured out a good way to light him when he was on TV—I mean when the combo was mixed.

"So how come Lord Randal here gets a dispensation?" Mr. Hippie kept on.

"Because he doesn't try to be black," said Mason. "He plays out of what *he* knows, and that gives us contrast. Most whiteys try to sound like they were brought up in sanctified churches. What they *do* sound like are the sons of mothers who had colored maids."

"You really do think it's possible to hear black," Mr. Hippie said.

"Man," said Mason, "I can *always* tell if a black man's playing."

"I got fifty bucks that says you can't make twelve out of twelve."

"OK. Your move."

"Ten minutes," said Mr. Hippie. "Give me ten minutes." And he ran out the door. The club, the Blue Note, was way west near the Hudson, below the Village. Mr. Hippie lived nearby on Vandam Street. It took twenty minutes, but he was back—with a battery-powered phonograph and a batch of LPs. He put on one after another, keeping score with a pen on a bartab, as Mason said, "Black, black, white, black, white." After twelve solos, Mr. Hippie threw his pen down with great glee. "Fifty bucks," he shouted. "You owe me fifty bucks. You were wrong three out of twelve."

Mason didn't even bother to check, to look over the records. He took out five tens, threw them on the bar in front of Mr. Hippie, and picked up his case.

"Well," said Mr. Hippie. "What happened to your black ear?"

Mason looked at him, his face blank. His eyes were nearly closed though, and he was speaking very softly, so I knew he might go up in the air any second. "What happened was I underestimated how good copiers you white bastards can be. That's all. The Japanese do it with radios; you mothers do it with our music. But that's OK. Times have changed enough so that the soul-slummers want the real thing. They want black in front of them. He," Mason looked at me, "is working for *me*. The next stage," Mason looked at Steve, "is black behind the cash register. All the way behind."

Mason left, and I had no interest in playing colored ticktacktoe with Mr. Hippie. I finished the bourbon and walked out. Usually, at this time on a Wednesday night, there was no one in sight. But across the street, in a triangular patch of cracked concrete with three benches, there were maybe twenty people. And a patrol car. As I walked over, one cop was pushing the sightseers back and the other was looking up the street. Waiting.

I peeked through a hole in the bodies and saw a big, broad cat, stretched out on a bench. There was a knife in his throat, blood down his chest. I leaned forward, and, before getting elbowed in the head by the goddamn cop, I saw his face. It was that son-of-a-bitch Sanders, the plainclothes cop.

Who said there wasn't justice on earth?

5

Billy

All wasted. I'd spent half the night trying to figure
out ways to bug Sanders real good. Coolly, you know, like
from a distance. Like from nowhere so I don't get involved.
And I pick up the *Daily News* and the bastard is dead.
Damn! Here I'd had something to focus on. All that pleasure in anticipation gone. Just like the bastard. Getting himself killed to deprive me of my kicks. Shee-it.

Day off. And nothing to do. Nothing I wanted to do. I
almost would just as soon have been working. Being an engineer at the station was cool. Mostly I taped and edited,
and some of the programs were even worth listening to.
WRQW was just FM and had no commercials. "Listener-
sponsored radio" was the bit. Cats sent in fourteen bucks a
year because we gave them some things they couldn't hear
anywhere else. And in a way we did. At least we gave them
more jazz and more folk music than anybody else. And a lot
of lectures and symposiums—and Thomas's documentaries.
And comment. Jesus, enough comment to stock a dozen
scrawny magazines. Birchers and Maoists and liberals and
black nationalists and even one old-timey Commie. About
all we were missing were Rosicrucians and astrologists.

Ten in the morning and a whole day and a whole night to kill. I picked up the *Times,* the *Tribune,* and the *News* and read every word about Sanders getting it. And then I read the stories again. Who was the hero? What a shame the cat couldn't announce himself. I bet you could have filled a big hall with people wanting to give a testimonial dinner to whoever did it. It wasn't that Sanders had just been a bastard. It was the cat was all evil—all over evil. He could just say, "Hello," and you'd start sweating and want to throw up. And being a cop, there was nothing to hold him back. You knew that if he wanted to he could eat you up. That was it, he was like a big, black lizard you could never get away from. Now I missed him. Having all that evil right in front of you was more satisfying—scared as you could be—than just getting it in bits from other people. With Sanders you knew where you were. He couldn't surprise you by changing his nature. That's a comfort, you know. He was like an absolute. Like Greenwich time. Like death, if you believed in death. Yeah, I was beginning to miss him.

There was bony John the Avenger, crossing Second Avenue like a walking spear. He was grinning all over about Sanders, but after I talked to him awhile, he was missing him too.

"I hadn't thought of it that way," John shook his head. "You live in a jungle, it helps to know exactly where you're at sometimes. You hear what that boxer with that mean mustache said in the paper, the guy that's fighting at the Garden Friday? 'Life is nothing but a jungle. If you don't watch out, some cat's going to jump down out of a tree and eat you up.'"

"I was thinking just that about Sanders."

"Yeah, but like you were saying, he wasn't up any tree. And he wasn't any symbol. He was him. And you could hate him right in the face and in the body. And—" John grinned, "he was one black man you could hate without feeling like you were in some way betraying the members. You could hate him white. Because he was like a black man they'd turned inside out. Yes, he served a valuable function. I bet some paddy killed him because they forgot he'd turned white."

"Hell, any color could have killed him, and all the ones in between. I figure we'll never know."

"I will," said John. "I got to know. I got to know all these interconnections. You never know where the key is gonna come for the next door."

"Key?"

"To power, man. Who wanted Sanders killed? What did Sanders know? It could lead right up into one of those concentric power structures."

"Now just suppose he was collaring some half-ass hustler, and the cat just didn't have the time to lay over at the Tombs. It could have been as simple as that."

"Few things are simple—if you dig hard enough."

"Good luck, John. I bet you never figured you'd be Sanders' avenger."

"Fuck you, Billy." He said it affectionately, you know, and walked by.

"Oh," John turned around, "one thing. Septimus is back."

"The black Dostoevski?"

"Yeah. He came by this morning for some bread and a place to stay. Bread he got. He'll find you."

Damn. I'd lost track of time or he got a parole sooner than I'd figured. What was the last bit? Five years for almost taking that guy's head off. Literally. He almost cut his head off his body. Lucky for him it was a black junkie or he would have got a lot more. I never knew a cat who did more reading and more writing and who got into more trouble all at the same time. The two years I was at Fisk there was no one on that faculty who was anywhere near Septimus as a mind. I'd come home and, if he wasn't shut up somewhere, he'd talk Schopenhauer and Nietzsche and Sartre and Buber and Du Bois and God knows what else. And he'd show me a new story he'd written. Those stories could make you ice cold in the middle of July. Cats raping and killing children to redeem humanity. Cats stretching themselves as far as they could go and then snapping. I'd finish one of his stories and Septimus would lean over, "What do you think?" "Crazy," I'd say. And I meant it. Both ways. Then he'd disappear for a few days in Brownsville or Bedford-Stuyvesant and come back greasy and gray. As gray as someone that dark brown could be. I once asked him what he did those times but he snarled at me like a jaguar, so I stopped asking.

I came back to the apartment, and Dianne was in bed.

"You're not working today?"

I looked closer, and she'd been crying.

"Sanders," she said.

"So?"

"I was mean to him."

"Oh, boy, you feeling guilty? He made you sick!"

"Yes, but did I really know him? Did I let myself get to know him? Who knows what was deep inside there?"

"Spiders," I said. "And slugs and squirmy snakes and a man-eating frog with one big, horrible eye."

"No, no. Nobody's all black."

"Watch your self-image, baby."

"There's no talking to you."

"You can talk to Septimus. He's back."

She shot up all stiff and opened her mouth but didn't say anything. For a second.

"He is NOT going to stay here."

"He hasn't asked yet."

"He will. I am not having that psychopath in this house."

"Did he ever hurt any of us? He goes somewhere else when he's acting up."

"Acting out." She couldn't resist showing those courses in psychology. "That's like having a dog with rabies in the house who hasn't bit anyone at home—yet."

"Here you're bleeding about what was deep inside Sanders, and you *know* Septimus isn't all black—as you put it."

That stopped her. This was one of her mornings when she drank guilt instead of coffee. They didn't come often but they came. I pressed her. "Septimus is still alive. Not for long maybe. But he's breathing and walking and scuffling for a place to just sleep. You going to just send him away?"

She didn't say anything, and before Septimus rang the bell, I'd taken the folding cot out of the closet and put it in the small room off the kitchen I used to store things, and I put another glass in the bathroom.

"It's on you," she said, when the bell rang. "Whatever happens is on you."

"Don't worry, baby. I'll have you buried out of Community Church. With a white minister."

6

Dianne

When Billy said Septimus, he put me back eight years into that room at the Theresa Hotel. I'd just finished my first year at Smith and was all torn up inside. Torn up good and torn up bad. I'd been so damn *visible* there. Of course, she must be a scholarship student. Of course, we must be extra nice to her. Of course, all this must be a terrible strain on her. On us too, but we must extend ourselves to make up for the past. Of course, we ought to ask her home, but then, she couldn't reciprocate, could she, so perhaps asking her would be too embarrassing? But I'd made it. Good grades. Good posture. Good show. And by being so cool, I'd put them as much on the defensive as I was. By the end of the last semester, a smile from me meant something to some of them. Like they'd made it too. They didn't have all the power. I had some in reserve.

Coming back home though was a drag. Oh, the apartment itself was all right. We lived on a "good" Harlem street—153rd off Amsterdam. And the place was big and clean. So goddamned clean all the goddamned time. Like it was on exhibit. But *I* was different. I'd been to another country. Whatever I told the girls I'd gone to high school with, they took as a put-down. "Well, we don't have con-vo-cations in the five-and-ten," Doris had said when I was try-ing to tell them about Ralph Bunche speaking at the school. And the boys either clawed at me from the first minute to show I was still just pussy after all or they looked down at their feet as if I had turned into a schoolteacher. Except for Septimus. He asked me about my courses and made me keep digging into what I thought I'd learned. He upset me that way. He asked questions I should have asked the pro-fessors. And he never once mentioned the race thing. He wanted to know what else I was putting in my head.

I knew what they said about him—mainly from Billy. That he was a hustler, a sometime pimp, a sometime thief, a sometime pusher. That he was dangerous, with or without a knife. That he could suddenly turn into an animal. That he'd been in Warwick and Elmira and Green Haven. But whenever I saw him, he spoke softly, hardly ever used street talk; and in his Brooks Brothers suits and horn-rimmed glasses he looked like a bank cashier on whom the manage-ment had its benevolent eye. Sometimes I tried to get him to talk about himself, but he'd only talk about what he'd been reading. Nothing else. He was always gentle with me, and I liked him, so I didn't care what they said.

One July morning, Septimus came by the apartment early. He was, in Billy's term, strung out. His suit looked as if he'd slept in it although *he* didn't look as if he'd had any sleep. His white shirt was filthy and, for the first time since I'd come home, I saw him without a tie. It seemed very odd, Septimus without a tie. Like a crack in a picture, a crack that grew longer as you kept looking.

He had on dark glasses, and although he kept staring at me, I couldn't, of course, see what was in his eyes. It was very disconcerting.

"Billy told you what I do—sometimes," he said as he came in.

"Yes."

"Well, it's true."

"Why is it true?"

"Take too long to tell you. Look up some texts on abnormal psychology, and we'll go from there."

After a silence, he said, "I want you."

"Just like that."

"It's not just like that. I'm not a stranger. We've got other things going between us. This would make it complete. That is, if you've got that kind of feeling too."

I wasn't used to anyone like Septimus being that direct. The guys in the neighborhood *were* strangers to me now, and their "courting" was so blunt that it was easy to straight-arm them without even talking. Just a look and a drawing back. The middle-class boys, both the few at home and the ones who came to Smith for dances, were all more or less the same. They'd take so long to talk you into bed that I had no difficulty sidetracking them any time I wanted to. But with Septimus, all our talk had been about books and ideas until that morning. I wasn't prepared for his putting it to me so straight without any preliminaries at all.

"Well, do you?"

It was weird. I just said, "But not here."

"I have a room at the Theresa. Let's go."

I went into the bedroom for my diaphragm, put it in my bag, and we left. We didn't say a word until we were in the room. The walls were gray; there was a stringy gray-and-white bedspread on the bed; and Septimus seemed gray. He was trembling a little, and I saw his hands had tightened into fists. We undressed; Septimus pulled down the shades.

"Please take off those glasses," I asked.

"Do I have to?"

"Yes, damn it. I don't want to be the only one naked."

He took them off, and I wished he'd kept them on. He stared at me, just stared. Not at my body but at me—into my eyes.

We got into bed, and he started shaking. I ran my hand over his shoulders, his back, and then between his thighs. There was no erection. Suddenly he grabbed me hard around the waist, lifted me on top of him, and squeezed so that I could hardly breathe. I felt no stiffness as he tried to get inside. He let go and got up so fast I was dumped onto the bed.

He stood, his back to me, banging his fist into his hand. "I knew it," he said. "I knew it. I'm just a goddamned case history." He dressed fast, put on his glasses, and stood by the door.

"You're just going to leave me here?"

"You're lucky, baby. Last night I banged a whore so bad —inside and outside—she's not going to work for a while."

"Septimus, at least talk to me."

He took out his knife; I heard a click; saw the long blade; and almost the instant I saw him throw it, I heard it stick and shiver in the headboard just above my head.

"I wasn't trying to hit you," he said, and walked out.

I'd seen him off and on since then. Never alone any more. And what little we'd say to each other was perfunctory. And I kept hearing the stories about him. Until he went back to prison. From there he began sending me letters about what he was reading, thinking, writing. About his having one more chance before he'd become a criminal all the way. About how he wasn't at all sure that chance was worth taking.

In one letter I kept, he'd written:

It's quite probable I'm conning myself two ways. First, I'm a psychopath. Whether "society" made me one or not, that's what I am. In a way, it's like being an epileptic. How will I ever know when I'm going to have a "seizure"? How can I ever trust anything I do, particularly in terms of finishing it the way I'd intended?

And then, aside from myself, can this life that man has made for himself—this jungle, whether you're talking about this country's foreign policy or the cats on Eighth Avenue—ever be anything else but worse? The Western ethical tradition—from the Greeks to Sartre and Camus —is know yourself, *be* yourself, even if there is no rational design for the rest of it. Even if the rest of it is absurd. But why? Isn't that another kind of cop-out? Another kind of self-conning? If the rest of the world is irrational, is murderous, what will you find if you *do* go down all the way and "know" yourself. More irrationality. More murderousness.

No, what that sermon always means is: *you're* different. You've got potential to transcend whatever there is in you of the cancerous rot of the world. Fulfill that potential, baby, and you'll be like a model for mankind. I've made it, Jack, follow me. And some of these children of Socrates go a step beyond. If I know myself, they say, I can change the world. I can like start a revolution by getting other cats to know themselves. Shit.

You remember the diabolical Herr Naphta in *Magic Mountain*? "No," he said, "liberation and development of the individual are not the key to our age. They are not what our age demands. What it needs, what it wrestles after, what it will create—is terror. . . . Only out of radical scepsis, out of moral chaos, can the Absolute spring, the anointed Terror, of which the time has need." Now that's crap too. We already have it. The moral chaos. The Terror. Anointed too. "Free world Terror." "War of National Liberation Terror." "Fuck whitey Terror."

So what if *this* is the Truth? Violence. Terror. Then, if

you go all the way with that, you *are* knowing yourself, you *are* fulfilling your real potential. And what is real is taking, raping, killing, fulfilling the Absolute, the only Absolute—that we're animals, baby, and the rest is a con.

So, which is true? Is there a beast in me that can never be exorcised? Is there a beast in me that *can* be exorcised —by, like psychiatry or self-confidence through making it "straight"? Or is the beast the world and the world the beast? And we're all part of the terror that is man. And we devour each other as we ourselves are devoured, either from within or without.

Let me know when you find out.

He sent me a few more letters like that, but my answers were always brief and not to the point at all. Just, "You've got the potential to do whatever you want to do. You'll make it when you get out." Jive like that. I just couldn't meet him on his own ground. I'm not equipped. And maybe I'm scared. Maybe I just don't want to look that deeply into life. Certainly not into his life. Anyway, after a few months, his letters stopped.

Septimus came by early in the afternoon. Billy had to talk to him for an hour to persuade him to stay, that he wasn't inconveniencing us. Septimus finally asked me if I minded. "You heard Billy," was all I said. And he stayed. And I'm scared.

7

Thomas

Sanders' murder was an enormous relief to me. I knew that, one way or another, he would have gotten me. Not killed me, but close enough. The last time I'd seen him—a week before he was killed—he'd come over to the table at the Blue Note, while Dianne was in the ladies' room.

"You don't listen good," he'd said.

I'm no hero. My heart began to pound as if it wanted to get out of a disaster area. Out of me. But I tried to play it cool.

"So long as I don't break any law, Sanders, all you can do is talk."

That voice of his, sounding like a frog under water. I bet all they had to do at the precinct house to crack a guy was turn down the lights and just let Sanders talk. And his laugh, which was what he was doing then, was much worse. It wasn't a laugh really. It was a hungry growl of expectation, like he could already feel his hands digging into me. Finally he stopped laughing.

"You're so square, boy, you're only half a mother-fucker. You just go on thinking that. You just go on not breaking any laws. Of course, you don't know *all* the laws. I make up new ones every day. And the punishments that go with them."

So, when I saw his corpse lying all over the front page of the *Daily News*, it was as if a doctor had called me and said he'd made a mistake, I didn't have cancer after all. But the murder kept gnawing at me. More violence. The city was turning into a giant laboratory to prove Hobbes's description of the natural state of man. People were tearing at each other—stealing, raping, killing. We'd all been thrown into Alley Oop's strip, and the time machine had broken down, leaving us back with the dinosaurs—and each other.

I decided to do a series for the station on violence in the city. Verbal violence of all kinds. I heard it like a terrifying, dissonant prelude to Armageddon. Of course, there would be a nuclear war. Man being what he is, he *had* to use every weapon he had. Sooner or later. I fantasized a new race of men—or maybe explorers from another planet—coming upon my tape in the ruins of the city a thousand years from now. They listened to it. They didn't need a machine. They had all kinds of built-in sensory apparatuses.

"Oh," one of them says, "I see now. It's perfectly clear."

"Yes," says the other, "isn't it remarkable they lasted so long."

"Well, the universe is well rid of them."

"Think of the challenge though. Perhaps we could have changed them, reconstructed them."

"No. No. Listen to them again. No. They were animals. They could only be civilized up to a certain point. A very low stage of civilization. And it never held. The animal kept breaking through the crust. The only thing to have done if we had confronted them at the time was to destroy them. Chronic menaces, every one of them. Fortunately they saved us the trouble."

I decided to ask for Billy as my engineer. He was hip, cool, and he'd have ideas of his own on what we ought to include.

"This is just a beginning list," I told him. "Mothers and their kids. All over the city. All kinds of different neighborhoods. Cops. John the Avenger."

"And," said Billy, "we can go out to Queens and tell some of those white mothers we're doing a survey about busing their kids into black schools."

"One whole hour should be of marriages. We got to get everybody we know telling us where to take the tape recorder. Like, in my building, a Chinese couple erupts about midnight practically every night."

"There's a couple of mixed marriages we can use," said Billy. "You're not going to edit out things like 'white bitch' and 'nigger'?"

"No, this is sociology, man. Public service documentary sociology. We're giving mankind a last chance to save itself. To look at that naked lunch on the end of the fork."

"Uh-huh," said Billy. "Nonetheless it could be fun. When do we start?"

"Tomorrow night. A friend of John has a new play opening on Second Avenue. I've seen part of the script. It makes Jimmy Baldwin sound like Martin Luther King. I got permission to tape the whole thing and then we can pick what we want."

"OK. Meanwhile I'll start working on the marriage bit. That part really moves me."

"There's nothing that gives an unmarried man more pleasure than to hear a husband and wife going after each other's entrails."

"Yeah, man. That's what I mean."

"Monday we'll make Washington Square Park for the mothers and the kids."

"And the kids with the kids. We'll tape some of the scene in the sandbox."

8

Randal

Off night for us was Monday so I went along with
Thomas and Billy to the play. Dianne came too, and a guy
named Septimus Williams. About Billy's age, thirty-two or
thirty-three. Black. Really dark brown. A little less than
medium height. Compact, but just barely. I mean he looks
like he was about to burst. With energy, with muscles.
And he's also just barely contained in other ways. He talks
soft but clipped and there seem to be more words pushing
to get out than he's going to allow. And there's the feeling of
something else inside him straining to get out. I can't put
what that is in words. Mainly because I don't want to.

We walk in, and Septimus elbows Billy.

"There's that mother-fucker Horowitz."

"The cat that sent you up the last time?"

"The same." They were looking at a little man, maybe five
four. He was very neatly dressed. And hot as it was that
August night, he looked as if he'd no more sweat than ever
wear a sport shirt. He was thin, his face was thin, his eyes
were thin. But he wasn't brittle. He was like a knife blade.
He saw Septimus and came over.

"Ah, Williams. Good to see you out."

"Fuck you, Horowitz."

Horowitz frowned. "Of course, I understand your malice. But as I recall, you're also very sophisticated. Surely you know I had no vengeful pleasure in apprehending you or testifying against you. A gig is a gig."

"Yeah, but why *this* gig for you? Being a cop obviously fills some need in you. A lot of needs."

"I'm disappointed, Williams. Such oversimplification. I will grant that subconsciously some of what you say is likely to be true. Let us say it is. But I gratify my quotient of sadism, of aggression, of ordinary human meanness in a manner that is of social use. Most of the rest of humanity does not. I refer not only to criminals, but to husbands, fathers, businessmen, lovers, what have you. Having no socially approved—and socially relevant—way of indulging in their—uh—cop instincts, they exercise them in subterranean ways. And that leads to transmogrification of already dangerous impulses."

Dianne was uncomfortable. She tugged first at Billy and then at Thomas to move away from Horowitz and go to their seats. But both were rooted. So was I. Septimus, his face impassive, rocked slightly on his heels.

"There is a further point," Horowitz went on. He lowered his voice, almost to a whisper. "I do not expect you to know this," he looked at Septimus, "because you do not know me. We met only as quickly passing adversaries. But, in fact, I chose police work deliberately because so few men like myself do become policemen. I reveal no secrets in describing the vast bulk of the force as composed of insensitive men. Insensitive to the ambivalencies endemic to every choice in life. Insensitive not only to the effect of, let us say, race prejudice on both victim and daily executioner, but insensitive to all manner of other forces in this exceedingly complicated society with its limitless shades of gray. Therefore, it became clear to me that if this socially essential instrument—the police—were to be more than a mindlessly brutalizing bludgeon to maintain simple order, it was my responsibility —my moral responsibility—to become part of it and help in its transformation."

Septimus grinned. "You are something else."

"Mind you," Horowitz nodded, as if Septimus had applauded him, "I recognize fully that my aim in this regard is essentially futile. I have been in the department for ten years and know of only perhaps six or seven men with my moral concerns. My moral sensibility, if you will. However, as an existentialist, I long ago accepted the challenge of Camus. Realizing the ineradicable absurdity of life, I could either commit suicide or commit myself to my values, as difficult of attainment outside of myself as they are. But I must admit I had no idea of how unchallenging police work soon becomes. I may soon have to try to be useful in some other function."

The buzzer sounded, and the lobby began to empty. "I've enjoyed this," said Horowitz. "Perhaps we might have a drink some time."

"Yeah," said Septimus. This time Horowitz couldn't have misinterpreted his grin. "I'll name the place."

"Of course," said Horowitz, "I am also a fatalist, and no longer anticipate fear. Which I rather regret. Fear, or certain kinds of fear, can, as I recall, be delicious."

The audience was as mixed as any I'd seen. Uptown white hippies, wanting to be in on the newest turn of the knife in the white psyche. Local black Zionists. Mixed couples. Black and white. White and black. And some homogeneous. White and white. Black and black. Faggot and faggot. Lesbian and lesbian. I recognized some writers. And actors. And John the Avenger. And for once, I couldn't play my game of locating the fuzz. Horowitz, in the third row, had a notebook on his lap and was already writing, looking around the room from time to time. He was casing the audience too.

The play began a drag. The first stages of the revolution after the blacks had won. Mopping up. All kinds of tribunals with all kinds of white criminals. All of them got executed after getting verbally violated. The dialogue was mainly variations on playing the dozens with each criminal. Fuck and mother-fucker and shit were like punctuation. One black leader spoke at one point of this being the last transition stage before the new society would begin. The black vanguard first had to get the last cancerous rot out. And then the fucking and mother-fucking and executing continued.

I fell into a doze but jumped awake when I felt a gun against my forehead. A goddamn actor had moved up the aisle, picking out the criminals in the audience. The writer had seen *The Blacks*. "And you, the slavemaster," he yelled at me. "You who slept with our women—"

"And smoked your pot," I said.

"You will be buried alive in your own shit. You will die as you have lived."

He moved on, shaking his gun at another white. Billy was on the right side of the stage, grinning, huddled over the tape recorder. Thomas was taking notes. Dianne looked nauseated but also fascinated. There was no telling what Septimus was thinking.

At intermission, before we could talk about the play, Horowitz walked over. "Very significant," he said to Septimus. "Bad art, but important."

"How come you're here?" Septimus asked.

"Well," Horowitz was mildly offended, "I go to plays all the time. Especially plays that reveal the strains in the society. But actually, tonight I'm here on business. I'm on loan to the Department of Licenses."

"You mean your job is to say whether the show gets busted?"

"Not exactly. I simply make my recommendation and then the Commissioner decides. But he has great faith in my ability at this. He knows of my background. I did my graduate work in sociology, you know. And my major as an undergraduate was English literature."

"What's the verdict?"

"Oh, no question about it, the play has every right to continue. There is obscenity, to be sure, but it is entirely within the constitutional use of obscenity according to the most recent Supreme Court decisions. The play is making social comment. The obscenity isn't being used for its own sake. No, this isn't hard-core obscenity at all. Perhaps now you understand more of what I was saying before. If an ordinary inspector from the License Department had been sent down, the play would have been closed instantly. But fortunately, I'm the inspector; and fortunately, I do have the capacity to distinguish between serious—if amateurish—art and dirt."

"Horowitz," said Septimus, "do you believe in the concept of justifiable homicide?"

Horowitz frowned. "I'm afraid I've missed the connection. What has that to do with—"

"Forget it," said Septimus, and started to move away.

"No, no," Horowitz followed. "I'd like to answer."

"Forget it, you mothering Jew," said Septimus, and started toward his seat. Horowitz stiffened for an instant, then smiled, and was cool again.

"Hey, man," Billy caught up with him, "that was beautiful."

Septimus grinned.

"You got him feeling comfortable, and then you kicked him in the balls."

"He's going to have more fun and games," said Septimus, "before we're through with each other."

John the Avenger was ahead of us, looking gleeful.

"That play is telling where it's at," he said to Billy and Septimus, nodding toward the stage.

"It's shit, John," said Septimus. "It's doing stunts for whitey. Plays like that are the new horror movies. Whitey goes, lets himself get nice and scared, eating fear like candy, because he *knows* there ain't any Dracula. And there ain't any black revolution. Clowns. You're all clowns, still tumbling for Charlie."

"You're wrong, Septimus." John was hurt. For a second, his lower lip came out like he was going to cry. "There *is* a revolution starting, Septimus. I'll show you." John reached into a coat pocket, looked at me, and stopped.

"You think this guy is the man from U.N.C.L.E.?" Septimus smiled at John like he was a kid, a little kid.

"Randal's better than most," said John, "but it's too late for anybody his color."

"You guys ought to sell life insurance on the side," I said. "You collect the premiums, and then when you win, there'll be none of us left to pay off."

John wasn't amused. Septimus looked at me like he couldn't quite figure me yet. We all went inside.

The second act was in exactly the same key as the first. More whites being judged, yelled at, and killed. More blacks stomping around, on the stage, up and down the aisles, poking guns into expectant white faces in the audience. Horowitz was industriously taking notes, Billy was rid-

ing gain on the tape recorder, Thomas was reading a maga-
zine, Dianne looked like she wished she were a full-blooded
Indian, and Septimus—

Septimus had been slouching in his seat, his eyes half
closed, when an actor, gun in hand, jumped in front of him.

"And you, black brother," the actor roared, "you too are a
witness to the end of white barbarism and the beginning of
civilization. The cycle of the spirit has entered the orbit of
healing, liberating blackness."

"But wait." Septimus got up like he had lines too. "We
haven't finished the preparations. There is still cancerous rot
to be cut away."

The actor was lost for a moment, but he decided to go
along with Septimus. "We know, brother, we know," he
said.

"There!" Septimus pointed at Horowitz five rows away.
"There is one of their leaders, one of the most treacherous of
the white devils."

The actors on stage froze like they were in a still shot.
Horowitz had turned toward Septimus and was smiling.

John the Avenger whispered to Dianne, "That's that goddamn cop, isn't it? The one that sent Septimus up?" Dianne
nodded. John stood up. "Yes," he began to yell, "his list of
crimes requires the slowest of deaths." John must have given
some kind of signal, because, immediately, four other Negroes in the audience jumped up, pointing hard at Horowitz. John slammed his way out of his row and moved toward Horowitz. So did Septimus. And the four others. And,
smirking at each other, figuring maybe this could be
more fun than the lines they had to say, the actors came toward Horowitz too. Down they came from the stage. Joined
by the one who'd stopped in front of Septimus, they ad-
vanced on Horowitz.

The cop sat there, still smiling, but no longer taking notes.

"Hey," I said to Thomas.

"Cool it," he said. "It's their ball game."

"But I don't think John and Septimus are playing."

"So?" said Thomas. "If they're not playing, you figure on getting into a race riot—on the wrong side?"

I looked at him. "You'd let them kill him?"

"Oh," said Thomas, "it won't come to that."

Others in the audience were also getting the sense that maybe this wasn't a play any more. Some of the whites started looking toward the exits. There were white couples on either side of Horowitz and each drew together, trying to get as far away from Horowitz as they could.

In front of Horowitz now were John and Septimus. Behind them John's four colleagues and ten black actors. Septimus grabbed Horowitz by the knot of his tie, yanked him up, and slapped him hard on the right side of his face, on the left, on the right again. There were tears in Horowitz's eyes, but no pleading. He looked straight at Septimus. I looked at Thomas, but he wasn't about to move. I'm no hero, so I didn't either.

"Anything you want to say before sentence is passed on you?" John shouted in Horowitz's ear.

"You," Horowitz had trouble breathing, "are"—he was looking at Septimus—"at the edge."

Septimus punched Horowitz in the nose, watched the blood spurt, and turned to his retinue. "We will pass sentence on this white devil later. But now, on with the play."

"Gee," said a voice behind me, "it's like Pirandello. You see," he was talking to a young wide-eyed blond girl, I saw as I turned, "it's like wrestling. That little guy who got hit, he had a capsule of ketchup in his nose."

Septimus went back to his seat. Reluctantly, so did John and the other four. Septimus had broken the rhythm of the adventure and John didn't know where to take it. John

glared at Septimus. Dianne looked at him in not quite terror. Fear but a whole lot of curiosity too. Thomas was fascinated. Billy was grinning. I felt sick. Sick at myself, for not
having moved.

The play splattered on, and stopped. Horowitz had kept
on taking notes, between putting his handkerchief to his
nose. There were spots of blood on his shirt, his suit, his
notes.

Outside, he came over to Septimus. "This should turn out
to be very interesting," he said, smiling. "Next time perhaps
I shall direct the scene."

"I got no rules, baby," said Septimus. "From the back is
no problem for me."

"Oh," said Horowitz, "you won't kill me. I'm too important to you." And then, honest to God, Horowitz bowed to
Septimus. And Septimus bowed back!

"Shit!" said John the Avenger, moving past them.

9

Billy

Septimus didn't come home with us that night. I figured he'd done the usual, holed up in Harlem or Bedford-Stuyvesant. Juicing. Fucking. Looking for blood. His blood. Anybody's blood. No point going after him. He could just as easily come up the side of my head as anybody else's while he was like that. Acting out, like Dianne says. Acting out, shee-it. He was a mean cat and when the meanness came on him, he went for the throat or the balls or the pussy. Like a damn werewolf. But always he tore up other blacks. Ain't that a hell of a note. I got to talk to him about that—when he's his other self. Maybe I ought to try to get him on pot. Cool him off.

Next day Thomas was puffed up with pleasure. I'd taped the whole thing between Horowitz and Septimus. "To hell with the play," Thomas said, those soft Jewish brown eyes of his bigger and hungrier than I'd ever seen them before. "Man, we even got the fist against the flesh."

"I thought this was going to be a documentary of just verbal violence."

"We take what we can get." Thomas was so excited he

was pacing in circles in the control room. He's going to fat, I thought, looking at the curve of the stomach through the Brooks Brothers chinos. Another five years, when he was forty, he'd finally spring for a custom-tailored suit so he could hide the bulge. Fat Thomas would be no different from middle-size Thomas. Who was Thomas? A maker of documentaries. Getting his kicks by listening in. By looking. Ripe and ready for the feelies. I was surprised he could get it up for Dianne. Did he get it up for Dianne? Who the hell cared? Who *was* my sweet sister? A legal secretary. Hot shit! The black girl in the Great Society. The thin black girl who puts herself to sleep with J & B. Us members buy the best brands.

Thomas told me to take the tape recorder over to John the Avenger. So I fell by late in the afternoon. John would just be getting up, I figured. And this wasn't one of his teaching nights. Lean John, giving the word on black literature to the wide white ladies who wanted to get with *something* and to the slender young white ladies who wanted to get with him. Shirley had made it. John was her degree. Now she was into graduate work. First-hand research. Watch the baby. Bend the twig. But which way? Watch out, you're going to break it. But the baby is too little yet to break. Who'll break first? Five to two on the little Jewish mother. But maybe not.

Malcolm's gone, and here is John to take his place. But what place? Who's listening? John the Avenger, general of the black armies. He's got maybe eight in the ranks now and only nineteen million to go. How long, baby? How long before the Urban League? Or maybe a professorship at NYU? What are you saying, John? I'm listening, but what are you saying?

When I came in, he wasn't saying anything. He was listening, with a big smile, to an Archie Shepp record. So was

Shirley, but she wasn't digging it. She was frowning, shaking her head, looking at John, frowning, and shaking her head again. That Shepp jazz, I admit, is something else. Sometimes it's so far ahead that if you're looking for any kind of a melody or any kind of a beat to tap your foot to, you get lost right in front. And beauty? Man, that cat can sound like he's being strangled or is strangling someone else. The sounds are like splinters. They hurt your head. And they keep hurting. My head anyway. I can make Coltrane and Rollins, but these new guys leave me. I don't mind music with balls. But I don't want it to attack me.

But long John, he looked like he was hearing the Truth. I went to the refrigerator for a beer. "Dig," he said after me, "he's gone beyond notes! He's gone into *sound*. He's getting sounds no one ever got out of a tenor before. Black sounds, baby, black life."

"We're not screaming *all* the time. We make some love too. Where's that?"

"*I'm* screaming all the time." John cut off his smile. "All the time. Inside. Even during love. Especially during love."

Shirley grunted. "Tell me," she said, "if this music is so black, how come so few blacks dig it? How come Shepp isn't making it big in Harlem? How come he only makes it with you hippies downtown?"

"How come? How come?" John mimicked her, his voice high and tight, like Shirley's voice when she was getting into an argument. "How come they ain't all got guns? How come they let cops beat their kids? How come they don't tear down those fucking precinct houses, stone by stone, and lynch those cops? How come they don't burn out those mother-fucking white stores, like they did in Watts? Because they've been brainwashed. Because they're afraid. Because most of them do think of themselves as niggers. Dumb niggers. Dumb animals. They can't stand hearing

Shepp. He comes out of their guts. I don't see you listening to those old Jewish cantors with their crying and carrying on."

"That's different," Shirley said. "That's all over for the Jews here."

"But it's not all over for us. We haven't even got far enough to look at ourselves in the mirror. To let ourselves scream. I don't mean gospel music. That's OK for where it's at. I mean prerevolutionary music." John grinned. "You know, war dances."

"How come," I couldn't stay out of it any longer, "you aren't uptown waking everybody up? Man, as often as you're on Lenox Avenue, you're a tourist."

"That'll change," said John. Shirley looked grim. "I'm going to make my move," he went on. She looked at him. He looked back at her, kind of sad. "Not you, baby. We were too soon."

"Jesus Christ!" She spat it out, got up, and went into the bedroom.

"Got to be done," said John. "We got to get something together uptown. A place to teach the revolution. To teach alternatives. Politics, yeah. But things got to happen before the people are ready for black politics. Trouble with Watts is they had no plans for after the burning."

"And you?"

"We're working on them. We're studying. Like next week we may have a chance to see that Cuban cat, Viera. They're *doing* it, man," said John. "Here, when the burning starts, it's going to last a long time. Look, in a country with such big odds against you, how do you get a real resistance movement going? You got to have something to resist, something right in front of you all the time, hour after hour, day after day. In the ghetto there's not enough of whitey to touch now. You never see the landlords. All you got are the

Jew merchants and the cops. And some welfare workers. But you burn enough and you burn long enough and then you got troops in there. Scared troops. Troops that are going to make mistakes so the burning will start again. And again. And by then, with organizers and a program, we'll have a resistance movement. And when the troops pull out, we'll finally have some black unity."

"And what's the program?"

"Black for black. They got us in the ghetto. OK, so we run that ghetto. We decide where the bread goes that comes in from the government. The more burning, the more bread to re-ha-bil-i-tate us. Then maybe we make the political scene. No more Raymond Joneses. No more Adam Powells. We put ghetto cats in. Trained cats. Cats who won't be bought off. And this gets going in other cities, other ghettos. And we federate, man. All the centers of black power around the country unite. Black federalism. That's where Muhammad went off the track. We don't want no 'black nation' in a couple of states. Not that we could get it, of course. That old man's a fool. But we can make ourselves a black nation spreading all through *this* nation. And then we breed, baby. Fuck birth control. You notice how whitey all of a sudden is for us getting birth control. He knows. That's another part of the educating we got to do. Fuck birth control. Just fuck!"

John laughed. He laughed so hard he even drowned out Shepp's squawking.

"Damn," I said, "I should have taken you down on the tape for that series."

"The hell you will," said John. "I ain't ready for jail. Cops get that tape, snip out here and snip out there, and they got me breaking some damn sedition law. Besides, why should I do anything for that white radio station? Why are you there, brother?"

"Because it makes no difference where I am," I told him, "so long as nobody bugs me. You're as much a fool as Muhammad. Power. Shee-it. You're a chief without any Indians, man. The government's going to up the welfare and fix up the houses a little, and all your Indians going to stay right where they are. On their ass. You saw them, saying, 'Yeah, that Malcolm is telling it like it is.' But you didn't see them join him."

"That's because he didn't have a program yet. He was getting there."

"Look, you want to say anything into this machine? Anything about violence? I got a job to do."

"Wait a minute," John whispered. "Put it on." He turned off the record player. "Shirley!" he yelled.

"Yeah." She came in.

"Tell the truth, baby," said John. "Why did you marry me?"

"Oh, come on."

"Tell it, baby."

"Because, goddamn it, I love you."

"Love what, baby? Didn't you think about bed, about a black man in bed, about getting it so big and deep that none of those other Jewish girls could begin to imagine what real balling was like?"

"My husband, the stereotype," Shirley said to me. "Johnny, what are you trying to do? Lay off."

John got up, grabbed her around the waist, pulled her in to him, rammed his mouth against hers, got his tongue in, and his hand under her ass, bending her over. She was trying to say something, but stopped, and fell into it, her mouth opening wider, her legs beginning to spread. John dropped her.

"God damn you," she yelled from the floor. Tears came. Big tears.

"See, baby," said John. "Rub a black prick against white pussy, and all the walls come tumbling down."

"You son-of-a-bitch. Did you tell your friend how you always come too soon? How all the kicks are for you? Black lover, Jesus! Black masturbator!"

"Come on, Billy," said John. "Nothing more disgusting than seeing a white woman cry. They don't know how, you know. They can only squeeze it out, a little at a time. They is not in touch with their feelings, man. They is all dried up inside. They is all white inside. No, they is all gray. Poor little gray girl. Who's going to want to touch her now?"

I took the tape recorder and went out with him.

"You think I'm a bastard, huh?" John turned to me as we hit the street.

I didn't say anything. I've seen enough married people claw at each other so as to have no opinions. Most of them seem to like being torn up. Bug and let bug, I say.

"I got to split," said John. "I can't have a white wife. Not where I'm going and with what I have to do. But I dig her. Another time maybe we could have made it. Only thing I can do for her now is to make her *want* me to split. So I got to make her hate me. And I got to make it so much a matter of pride that she can't go back on that hate. That's why I did it in front of you. That's why I'm going to tell her later it's on tape. That Thomas, he'll use this, won't he?"

"Well, man, I don't know. Some of that language is not for the FCC."

"If he doesn't," said John, "let me borrow the tape and I'll play it when some people are over. Her friends, dig?"

"Games, you're always playing games."

"That's what it's all about, baby. Games. And it's time we started winning some."

"What are *you* going to win if you dig her that much?"

"I got to sacrifice, man. I got to prepare the way."

"The black Jesus."

"No, man, the Avenger, remember? Those that come after me can have private kicks."

"What about the kid?"

"Sacrifice, Billy," he grabbed me by my tie. "Watch who you tell what you know. You can be sacrificed too, you know."

I chopped his hand away. "Baby, I don't get *involved*. In nothing. I just watch the games."

"Pretty soon," John looked down at me, "everybody is going to have to play. Choose your sides."

"I'll improvise, baby, when the time comes."

John smiled and walked away whistling that Charlie Parker tune, "Now's the Time." Thomas would sure like that tape. Shirley, you should have stayed in the Bronx. You came too soon. I began to laugh. I bet she wished she had one of those cantorial records now. All she had in that house was black wailing. She didn't come prepared for anything. Maybe improvising *was* getting too hazardous. Maybe I ought to choose sides. But hell, wasn't anything going to happen. The thing was never to forget that it was all games. Shee-it, I never have to go to a show. I just visit my friends. Then I go home, smoke some pot, and replay the scenes.

10

Dianne

Another nothing night. Thomas knew Billy would be out working so he came over to the apartment. Not that Billy would care who I was with and what I was doing. He'd just go into his bedroom and fool around with the short-wave radio. The only thing is I wish Billy would bring a girl home once in a while so it just isn't me "entertaining." I used to think he was queer. He'd hung around Mother so much. In fact, he reminds me of her. So cool all the time. Only way you can tell he's really angry about something is when he starts to talk very, very slowly. Like she did. "Black people talk too loud," she'd say. "Like your father. That subway guard," she'd spit out his job. "He sounds like a train all by himself." And Billy's neat, like her. It's hard to imagine Billy without his pants pressed and his shoes shined. But he'd hardly ever go out on dates, and I never heard him talk about girls. Then I found out he picked up hookers. Pretty expensive hookers, white in the East Side clubs and black in places he knew uptown. "It's fast and clean," he said. "You never get bored with the same fox that way, and they got no claims on you. You buy what you feel

in the mood for, and when you don't feel in the mood, nobody's around pulling at you."

When I found my own place on Bleecker Street, he talked
me into splitting the rent. I didn't mind really. I hadn't
looked forward to living all alone, but I also hadn't wanted
any damn girl friend confiding in me. Billy was just right.
He was there and he wasn't there. Funny. We sure do take
after Mother. She never had any real friends either. Daddy
had so many he was hardly home. But she used to say it was
better to build your own inner resources so you didn't have
to depend on anybody for anything. Besides, she'd say, you
never can really trust anybody. They want to be your friend
only for what they can get out of you. But I just don't have
her inner resources, if that's what it is. I got to see some
people sometime. Even Thomas. Damn it, I stay alone too
much, I start eating at myself. And there's no taste.

So Thomas came over. With a quart of J & B to work on
I got high enough so I didn't care when he started to un-
dress me. That man sure enjoys touching me. And kissing.
Kissing me all over. I don't mind when there's enough
Scotch inside me. It's kind of interesting watching a man
get so much pleasure out of you. And the sounds he makes.
Like a starving man getting a big bowl of strawberries and
cream. OK, blackberries. But he can't make me help. He
begs, but I don't touch nothing of his. Let him do all the
work. He's the one getting the kicks. So he turned me over,
kissing my buttocks, and biting them. Very gently so I
didn't mind. My eye caught a *Daily News* by the side of
the bed with a story about the cops having no leads about
Sanders' murder.

"Hey," I said, "who do you really think killed that Sanders?"

He sat up, mad. Mad as hell. "What a cold bitch you
are."

"You want me, sweetie, you got to take me like I am." He hated my calling him "sweetie," said it sounded coarse. Jesus, but kissing my ass wasn't coarse. So he turned me over, got on top, pushed inside, and banged away. It began to be a little pleasant, but then he stopped. He'd had it. Well, it's still my clitoris, I thought. When he left, if I felt like it, I'd finish it.

So he lay there, breathing hard. I started to get up and put something on, but he pulled me down.

"Why do you let me do this?" he said. "Obviously you don't get aroused."

"I don't mind you, sweetie. And you're more or less normal. I don't figure you're going to beat me up or make me pee on you."

"Stop it, Dianne. You make sex sound so vulgar."

"It's not vulgar, sweetie. It just is. Some like it more than others. I don't mind it once in a while so long as I don't get mauled. You're a nice, gentle man. And you bring over good Scotch."

"Look, why don't we get married?"

"Don't be silly. What for? I don't want you in my bed every time I turn around."

"Good Lord, I mean more than sex. You know, kids, and being together."

"I don't want any gray kids. Black ones maybe some day. That's a beautiful color, black, you know. But of course, you know."

"But you're brown, and I'm not all that light."

Truth to tell, with his black hair and swarthy skin, he was one of the darker white men I'd known. But he couldn't ever have passed in my direction.

"Any way you look at it, they'll come out gray. If you're that anxious to contribute to miscegenation, there are a lot of black girls—brown, as you say—who'd like to marry a

nice radio station executive. Those who haven't turned nationalist yet."

"But you're the one I'm hung on."

"Sorry, sweetie, I'm for bed once in a while, but I'm not
for keeping."

Thomas began to drink. There was a third of a quart left
and it was all in him in about twenty minutes. I didn't want
him sleeping the night in my bed so I made him get himself
together and stumble out. I opened another bottle, but it
took a long time to get to sleep. Why did I let him munch at
me? Why did I see him at all? No inner resources. That was
it. No inner nothing. But what the hell, I'd known that for a
long time. Me and Billy were just cooling it. But it wasn't a
bad life. When I didn't stay alone too long. And maybe
some day some big black guy would find the way to unlock
me. I'm only twenty-six. There's time. I wondered what
Sanders would have been like in bed. Ugh. But maybe not.
Maybe he had something else, something Thomas didn't
have. He was a mean man, but he sure was a man. I bet I
wouldn't have had time to read the *News* when he was on
top of me. Too late. Too late. Sanders was dead. Who could
have killed him? Not Thomas, that was for sure. Septimus
could have killed him, but why? But Septimus wouldn't
have needed a reason when he was in one of his states. So
with Septimus on my mind I fell asleep.

The next morning in the office, I had a call. The voice was
vaguely familiar—soft but firm, kind of cultured.

"Miss Burnett, this is Mark Horowitz. We met the other
night under—uh—rather dramatic circumstances."

I said uh-huh and he asked if he could meet me after
work. "It's official business, in a way," he said, "but informal
official business. I shan't take much of your time."

What the hell, why not? Billy can't stand cops, but I don't
mind them one way or another. I told Horowitz to meet me

downstairs. I had nothing to do with the other girls in the office so they didn't know any of my friends to tell they'd seen me with a cop. If they made him as a cop anyway. There he was at 5:30. It was funny to look down on a man. I'm about two inches taller than Horowitz. He was cool. Those eyes. Green, and like neutral. Looking into those eyes, you couldn't tell what he was thinking or feeling. I doubted you could ever tell what that man was all about. One thing you could tell. He could take care of himself. That little man looked like he was made out of springs and steel. Steel springs.

I ordered a Scotch on the rocks and he asked for a martini. "Beefeater gin," he told the waiter. His gray suit looked expensive, soft and expensive. And I noticed the row of pens in his breast pocket. No ordinary ball points for Horowitz. A big fat black Mont Blanc, a silver Parker, and a thin gold Cross. Nothing but the best for Horowitz.

"Yes," he said, as if I'd asked him, "I believe in quality. There's no point in settling for the ordinary. But I come by my quality possessions honestly." He smiled. That is, his lips opened in a smile. But those green eyes didn't change. "There are those in my position who do quite well financially for certain special attentions to people in sudden difficulty with the law. But I find graft repugnant. It makes the receiver as well as the donor vulnerable. And we are all vulnerable enough, Miss Burnett, without making larger targets of ourselves."

I had some Scotch. And then I had some more.

"I asked to see you because I've been assigned to help out with the Sanders case. I have a particular expertise in certain areas in which he was working. You knew Detective Sanders, I know. In fact, he was quite fond of you, as I can well understand." He sort of half-bowed as he said that. Not a trace of a leer. "In my profession," Horowitz sipped his martini, "one has to be—or one ought to be—expert in judging people. Now, what I am going to tell you could constitute a mistake on my part, but I don't believe so. I am reasonably confident that you abhor violence and, more to the point, would abhor violence being done to you. And since you're an intelligent young lady, I'm confident you would do what you could to protect yourself."

"That sounds very much like a threat," I said. This was getting most uncomfortable. Maybe I'd goofed in agreeing to see him, but what the hell, he was a cop, and you can't escape seeing a cop if he wants to see *you*.

"Oh, no, it is not I who is a threat to you in any way. I'm speaking of your brother's friend—but not, I think, yours— Septimus Williams, who appears to board with you intermittently. I am not saying that Mr. Williams is a suspect, but he may become one. He knew Detective Sanders, as I expect you know."

I remembered. When Septimus was in his teens and Sanders was a patrolman on a Lenox Avenue beat, they'd had a run-in. Saunders had cracked Septimus's head. But I hadn't heard about anything else between them since then.

"I recognize that no decent person likes to be an informer, and a good thing that is too or we'd have a police state. I'm a civil libertarian secularist, you see, among my more zealous brethren who consider themselves ordained by an Old Testament God of Justice to extirpate evil by whatever means necessary. So I am not asking you to relay to me anything you may know or inadvertently find out that might possibly link Mr. Williams to the case. Nor certainly am I asking you to take part in any entrapment of Mr. Williams. I find that practice particularly abhorrent except when absolutely necessary.

"What I would appreciate is simply to know from time to time of Mr. Williams' whereabouts when he leaves your

apartment for any period of time. I know of his rather ec-
centric proclivities for losing himself, as it were, in Harlem
or Bedford-Stuyvesant during periods of—uh—stress. And
then it is very difficult to keep an eye on him. I'm not quite
sure how he does it, but he seems able just to vanish."

"In the first place," I told Horowitz, "I would have no
way of knowing where he goes. I don't know where he is
now. Second, I'd never ask him—"

"Because," Horowitz said softly, "you are trying to stay as
uninvolved with him as possible, a very wise course with a
man subject to seizures of violence. That, you see, is why I
feel it would be to your own interest to be sure that the unpredictable Mr. Williams is under constant, discreet surveillance."

I didn't pick up on that. "Thirdly, if I knew I wouldn't tell
you because by my definition, that would be informing
too."

"I understand your position and admire it. But just in case
an occasion may arise when, for reasons you cannot envision
at the moment, you might want to let me know where Mr.
Williams is, permit me to give you a phone number where I
can always be contacted quickly." He passed me a slip of
paper. My first instinct was to tear it up, but you know, it
could happen that with Septimus a time *could* come when
I'd want a cop fast. So I took the paper.

"And now that our quasi-social conversation is over,"
Horowitz signaled for another round, "would you like—I
know this is absurdly short notice—to have dinner with me?
And perhaps see that new Brecht production at the Cherry
Lane Theatre? I shan't be going in my functionary function." There was that smile again. I bet cobras, if they
smiled, would smile like that.

"No, thanks," I told him, and started to get up. That was
enough. A social conversation with Horowitz over another

drink was just too much after working all day. I needed to
unwind, not be wound up. He made me awfully uneasy because I felt he knew what I was thinking all the time.

"Of course," he rose too. "Perhaps another time. I have a
fair amount of free time evenings, and a very deep interest
in the theater. May I call you—unofficially?"

Well, why not? I'd never been out with anyone like him
before. Maybe he wouldn't seem as creepy off duty. So I
just nodded. He didn't ask for my home number. He knew I
knew he already had it. I swear I could feel him looking at
me, undressing me, as I walked out. I couldn't stop a shiver.
No, no date with Mr. Horowitz. That man almost made me
appreciate Thomas. Nice Thomas. Soft he was, but not in
the least dangerous. I hoped to hell he didn't call tonight.
All I wanted tonight was J & B and TV. Cozy. It really
wasn't such a bad life if you took care of yourself.

11

Thomas

I had the damnedest dream. I was in a car with Dianne and she was driving. But she wasn't driving. No one was. I got scared, realizing I was in the front seat all alone. Jesus, I don't know how to drive. I looked back and there was Dianne stretched out on the back seat—smoking and looking so damn pleased with herself. She looked back at me with that irritating smile she puts on just before she's going to call me "sweetie." And then we weren't riding any more. We were in her apartment and Septimus was there. Stamping his feet and complaining like a little boy winding up for a tantrum. Dianne was trying to soothe him, murmuring to him, trying to draw his head onto her lap. I was furious. There was something I *had* to tell her, something that couldn't wait, and she was paying no attention to me. I woke up, still furious. And hurt. And terribly lonely.

The hell with her. I had the series to work on, and that reminded me. Williams had to be part of it. I'd never met a man with so much violence in him. If I could get *him* going on what it felt like to be black, to be black in prison, to be black talking to me. But he hadn't reappeared yet.

"And when he does come back," Billy said, "I don't think

you're the man to talk to him. I can't exactly tell you why, but I think there's something in you that could set Septimus off, that could make him bang that tape recorder into your head. It's not just that you're white. I can see him talking to Randal and everything staying cool, but you're something else."

I was damn annoyed. "What kind of something else?"

Billy smiled. "Well, Thomas, nearest I can put it into words is that you're so soft and comfortable that when you come on probing at the private parts, so to speak, of somebody like Septimus, he's not going to be able to resist making you pay some dues so that you have the right to talk to him as if *you* were human. I mean, Thomas, I'm just role-playing. That's the way I figure Septimus would feel."

"Paying dues, paying dues. It's like a litany. I had no choice in being born white and middle-class. Am I supposed to invent stigmata, like some of those kids in the movement do? Have I ever come on patronizing or like a welfare worker? I'm the way with you or him that I am with everybody."

"That's right, Thomas. Who'd really mourn for you, Thomas? Whom would you really mourn?"

Oh, for Christ's sake. It was turning into group therapy. I'd had four years of *that*. You're not in touch with your *feelings*. You're all blocked up. And all that crap. Well, I function OK, and I don't harm anybody, and I'm not impotent. Even my ex-wife still likes me. So I'm not happy, whatever the hell that is. Who is? If I get very bugged, I can pour myself to sleep. I'm not so bad off. The nerve of that bastard. Who'd mourn for me? Who'd mourn for most people? Parents would mourn for their kids, but that's practically the same as mourning for yourself. One guy in a thousand might really mourn for his wife but that would be because she filled some big need in him—and that's the

same as mourning for yourself. All this rhetoric about giving
to people, communicating with people. Oh, once in a while,
I try, like with Dianne, but when it doesn't work, it just
means we don't have hang-ups that fit into each other. And
when it does work, it just means we've made a deal. I'll
make room for your neurosis if you'll be kind to mine. Jesus,
even Billy had started talking like Erich Fromm.

But all I said was "Look, Doctor, I'll take my chances.
Just let me know when he turns up again." Billy shrugged,
and did. A week later. "He's back at the house," he told me
in the control room one afternoon. "Give him a day to sleep,
and then call him if you still want to. Just don't interview
him there. I don't want blood on my rug."

I called the next day, explained what the series was all
about, and waited. There was silence for a few seconds, and
then Williams laughed, "You're a funny cat," he said. "You
going to codify all the different forms of verbal violence you
collect? You going to find a key to all that ails us all?"

"No, nothing like that." The only way to answer a put-on
is to be as straight and succinct as possible. "It's not going to
tell anybody anything they don't know," I couldn't help
going on, "but it may show people they're not as different
from everybody else as they thought."

"No shit! Imagine that. One big fucking, fighting family
under all the different skins. Man, how could I refuse being
part of so irrelevant a project? You have touched me at the
core of my being. Absurdity."

Screw the insults. He agreed to do it and we were to meet
at my place. I picked a night when Randal was off. Billy just
might be right, and I was in sufficient contact with my feelings to know I didn't want to get beaten up.

12

Randal

Septimus came in toward the end of the second set, sat in a booth, and nursed a beer. Mason nodded to him. I did too, but he looked back at me without showing any recognition. Too bad. The man intrigued me. The way he'd tried to shake up Horowitz at the play. Well, I figured, one whitey is the same as all whiteys to him. I understand that, of course, but it gets to be a drag. I used to keep trying to prove myself to that kind of guy, if I wanted to know him, but that was silly. It was like when I started playing, I used to try to play black. And that was sillier. Now I don't press any more, on or off the stand. If I come through as me, I come through. If I don't, it's no tragedy. By now I'm pretty straight as to where I'm at. In jazz, I'll never be a Wes Montgomery or a king of the new thing, but I'm better than many, white and black, and I get respect from the ones I respect. Like Mason. And otherwise I'm in pretty good shape. A nice pad of my own so far west in the Village it'll be a long time before they can raise the rent. Women when I need them. For an ex-junky and one of the last of the WASPs, I'm doing OK.

After the set, Mason sat down with Williams. I went to

the bar, had a bourbon, saw that super-hip press agent coming toward me and made for the door. But Mason called me over.

"Sit down if you've got nothing else going. This is Septimus Williams."

"We've met," I said. Williams looked at me. He looked amused.

"Septimus and I used to run together when we were kids," said Mason. "He wasn't a bad trumpeter."

"I knew my limitations early," said Williams. "When I was eighteen, too many kids younger than me were past me. But this one," he nodded to Mason, "took it like a religion. Of course, he had that thing, but nothing else seemed to interest him *but* music."

"Yeah," said Mason. "You get to know your horn, you don't need much else. Permanent, I mean. You can talk on it, you can talk to it, you can use it to tell if other guys really want to hear what you're saying. It's always ready for any way you feel. Of course, you can't fuck it. But that's about its only limitation."

"Remember," said Septimus, "how you used to hang out on that stoop on 153rd street just to see Coleman Hawkins come in and out?"

"Yeah. Bean was in last night." Mason smiled so Septimus knew what Hawkins had thought of Mason's playing. It had been near closing. Suddenly Hawkins was at the bar, his hat on the back of his head. Looking shorter, as he always does off the stand. Drinking cognac, and listening. We finished, Mason went down, and they shook hands. Hawkins nodded a couple of times, pointed to his ear, said, "I *heard*," and walked out. Mason was so pleased he bought the band —and Steve—a round.

"Septimus wants a job." Mason turned to me.

"What do you do?"

Septimus leaned back, finished his beer. "Well, just about anything. I cook, I lug furniture, I've been a book-store clerk, I can drive, I do carpentry. I don't much care what it is. I just want enough bread to eat, pay Billy some rent, and be able to write in some kind of peace."

"Music?"

"No, a novel, a play. I just have to write. You guys get it out your way, and that's mine."

"I know an actor who does carpentry for a living. Sometimes he has more gigs than he can handle." I gave Williams the guy's name and phone number.

"Thanks." He looked at me speculatively I guess you'd call it. "Mason tells me you both graduated from horse."

"Yup. He was a good example for me," I said, grinning at Mason.

"Shit. You didn't even know me then."

"No, but I heard how you holed up in Cleveland and sweated it out."

"Sweat wasn't all, baby. I was below the bottom then. But the whole thing was worth it, in a way. You get down that low, you look at yourself that low, and nothing about yourself is going to frighten or surprise you any more. It's no place to stay," Mason guffawed, "but it's a hell of an education being there. Right, Randal?"

"Yup." I didn't much like talking about it. Even with Mason. Sounded too much like AA heroics. I got hooked and I got unhooked. And that was that. I'd dropped out of college while I was on. That I regretted. And ever since I'd been off, I'd been thinking about going back. I wanted to be able to do something else if I lost it on the guitar. If I got to be old-timey. Or if the kicks just weren't there any more. But somehow I hadn't been able to push myself to go back. I had my days free, but I just never got around to make the move.

"I've been on from time to time," said Septimus, "but there were a lot of clean times." He smiled. "In the can. Finally it just got to be too damn much trouble. Too many cats can fuck you up. It's dangerous enough, as is, getting from one day to the next without putting that mark on yourself."

"That other mark," said Mason.

"Here's where I get drummed out of the club," I said.

"Shit," said Septimus. "I graduated from that too."

"Shall we make him an honorary brother?" Mason grinned.

"Sure," said Septimus. "That's the first belt, Randal. You get up to the fourth belt, you can call us nigger."

"South of Fourteenth Street," said Mason.

I saw Horowitz, standing near the end of the bar.

"Fuzz," I said to Mason. "The guy," I turned to Septimus, "you tangled with the other night."

"Horowitz. I suppose he wants a rematch."

"He was around last night," said Mason. "After you left, Randal. He's on the Sanders case. You knew Sanders, Septimus?"

"Yeah, I knew him. The walking nightmare."

"If I knew who knocked him off," said Mason, "I'd take care of his bar tab for a year."

"I can get very thirsty." Septimus smiled.

Mason frowned. I almost looked at Horowitz but jerked my head to the side and down.

"You just kidding, man," said Mason.

"Sure, Mason. Any way you like it."

We were due back on the stand, and as we went up the stairs, Mason said to me, "Don't jump to any conclusions."

"None of my business anyway," I said. And it wasn't.

When we were done, Septimus looked at his watch. "Got to split."

"I'll be seeing you tomorrow night," I said. "At Thomas's place."

Septimus grunted and then grinned. "You his body-guard?"

"If you'd rather, I won't show up."

"No, makes no difference."

When the next set ended, Horowitz was waiting for me in a booth. He didn't bother to introduce himself. Mason mumbled, "Mother," as he passed by. Horowitz looked after him without any apparent anger. "I imagine that made him feel good," Horowitz said. "Consider the variety of services we police perform. Convenient authority figures to swear at, to test one's manhood against. At a distance. Even, at moments of extreme catharsis, to kill. I confess I sometimes feel I'm ready for a change of vocation. Not that I mind the malice of some of the citizenry. But their expressions of it are so unimaginative, so predictable. As routine as police work itself."

I didn't say a mumbling word. "I notice you've added Mr. Williams," Horowitz went on, "to your admirably heterogeneous circle of acquaintances."

"Look, why waste time. I'm not going to be of any help to you for any purpose in any way."

"You know and I know," Horowitz spoke softly, "you have no right to a cabaret card. You have served time for possession of narcotics."

"Geez, after hearing you the other night, that's a pretty crude approach."

"Yes, it is indeed and I greatly regret using it. There are times, however, when one is limited in resources and those are the times, of course, when the spirit, if you will, of even the most conscientiously egalitarian police officer—so very few as there are—is further blighted. But we too must sacrifice bits of our virtue and our self-respect. It is that kind of world. Would that it were different. But, alas, counterforce is always necessary to pursue an objective successfully. And purely moral use of force is, alas, impossible. At least in my line of work. I wonder if Gandhi ever wrote of the applicability of soul-force in police work. I have not come across any such reference, but I suppose if one had been able to ask him, he would have replied that once the society and the people in it were changed through soul-force, why, then, there would be no need of police. But at the present imperfect moment, there is. Need of police, I mean.

"Consider the late Detective Sanders," Horowitz went on. I gave up and waved to Steve for a drink. "Many of his qualities were, to say the least, harmful to the creation of a somewhat better, more mutually trusting society. I mean Sanders not only as a policeman but as a man. Social forces had indeed distorted certain aspects of his character. It is no secret that he was, for example, brutal. I have stopped several of his interrogations, as a matter of fact, and thereby won, as it were, his enmity. And I am telling you no secrets, as an observant employee of this place, that he was dishonest." I looked toward Steve without meaning to. Sanders used to pocket at least fifteen bucks a week from Steve, and he'd always had a very big Christmas here.

"So we are not talking of the murder of an exemplary citizen. But we are talking about murder. And I'm sure I don't have to tell you that murder simply can't go unpunished for very basic reasons of our mutual self-interest. The social contract is tenuous enough, and in this city is becoming quite ragged. If we become permissive about murder, none of us is safe at all—not, I admit, that any of us is particularly safe as it is. This is all so obvious, I know, but there are times when the obvious becomes hidden in a mesh of individualistic imperatives—not wanting to be a fink, contempt for the police as authority. All too justified contempt, in many cases. Tell me, if you saw a truck run down a pedestrian and leave him bloody and broken, would you not take down the license number? I'm not even weighting my argument by making the victim a five-year-old."

"Yes, I'd take down the number if I saw it."

"And give it to the police."

"Yes."

"The situation with another kind of murder is basically the same, isn't it?"

"I suppose so."

"Forgive me this lecture and forgive me, if you will, my reference to your cabaret card. I simply wanted to make the nature of my task clear. I do not pursue the murderer out of any sense of vengeance. In many ways, we are all better off without Detective Sanders. But I do pursue the murderer for a very logical, communal purpose which, I believe, you now comprehend."

"Uh-huh."

"Has Mr. Williams said anything to you about Sanders?"

"Not a thing."

"A pity. I'm expert in detecting lies. I have to be, in my craft. Just as you have to be able to hear chords. You know, we can never have a rational society so long as people like yourself—with the capacity for clear thought—insist on being irrational. All right, I shall see you again. That was a very good solo, by the way, on 'Django.' Much better structured than on the record of it you made."

I felt like throwing up. Partly at Horowitz and partly at myself because the son-of-a-bitch had gotten to me with that goddamn corny lecture on civics. WASP keeps spelling square, I guess. Next thing you'd know I'd start each set with "America the Beautiful."

And that's all Mason would have to hear, that I had finked on Septimus. Mason and I had a social contract too and that was more important to me than the abstract one Horowitz was talking about. Hell, that wasn't all of it. I wasn't as self-reliant as I'd thought. There weren't that many people I cared about, and I'd lose every one of them if I became Horowitz's responsible citizen. One way or another, we're all accomplices. Shit, how the hell can you stay clean?

Horowitz had left a buck tip. Steve came over, picked it up, and tore it in two. I looked at him.

"I have to give those bastards money, but I don't have to take it from them."

"Is *he* on the take?"

"No, not him. That makes him much more scary. He wants something else."

"Like what?"

"Like blood. He makes me very queasy because he *is* honest. Ain't that something? A guy gives you the chills because he's *not* on the take. It's like he's not human. Do you know what I mean?"

I didn't know what anybody meant. Rather, I didn't want to think about it. I asked Steve to sell me a fifth of bourbon and I went home to my nice pad. I put on an album by Jim Hall and stared at the wall for a while. It really wasn't any of my business whoever had killed Sanders. But what about that truck? What about the sanctity of human life? I'm against capital punishment, right? But can I just walk away from Sanders the victim? What about Auden:

> There is no such thing as the State
> And no one exists alone;
> Hunger allows no choice
> To the citizen or the police;
> We must love one another or die.

That used to mean something to me, but what *does* it mean? There *is* such a thing as the State and Horowitz is it and all I know has taught me to keep away from it and him. And I do have a choice. I decide whom I love and whom I don't. It's absurd to talk about loving everybody. More rhetoric. More abstract nothing. There is no way for me to love Horowitz. I know that as instinctively as I know Monk is a great pianist and Oscar Peterson just plays the piano. And I am fond of Septimus. Besides, what the hell do I know? Nothing. Except that I *feel* he killed Sanders. And I could no more help Horowitz pin it on him than I could shit in the middle of the street.

It's weird. Horowitz did get to me about having a responsibility that murderers don't get away with it, and that shows one kind of decent impulse in me. I'm not all locked in myself, like Thomas. Like Mason in his way. But the fact that I'm not going to do anything about it, even if I did find out something that really tied Septimus in with the murder, shows another kind of decent impulse, right? Are they irreconcilable? In this case, yes. That's all there is to it. So right away, of course, I fantasize Septimus in a truck rolling over a five-year-old.

I wondered if Horowitz would do anything about that cabaret card. Or would he let it hang over me for a while? Nothing ever stays straight long. No one ever stays clean. I looked at my guitar on the bed. Nothing. Mason could get a fix from his horn any time he wanted to. I guess I didn't have the religion. Maybe I ought to get out of this. Do something *for* somebody. Teach. Something. I started on the bourbon, and sooner or later, I passed out.

13

Billy

I was leaving the station. It was around nine o'clock, a warm but not sticky June night, and I figured I'd walk the twenty or so blocks home. But there was John the Avenger waiting for me.

"How'd you like to meet Rafael Viera?" The Cuban cat he'd said he might be able to get to see. He'd been traveling through Africa and was in New York for some kind of United Nations scene.

"Sure. How come?"

"It's been arranged. What I need you for is to tape it— without him knowing about it."

"I thought he was one of your boys."

"That's not the point. I want to make sure I get everything he says and this is the only way to do it. Here." He gave me a very small tape recorder, a Japanese make I hadn't seen before. It was about four and a half inches long and two inches wide. "And four reels," John passed them over. "They last about a half-hour a side."

"I know. They run at one and seven-eighths. Yeah, I could keep the reels and recorder in my pocket and change them by touch. You'd lose maybe twenty, thirty seconds each time."

"That's OK. We go *now*."

Well, I was curious to see Viera, and I doubted if I could get busted taping a conversation with him. I'd probably get a medal if the Federal fuzz ever found out. We hopped a cab and got out on the east side of Madison and 67th. I followed John into a bar. Waiting for us were two of John's guys; a white cat from the Progressive Labor Party whom I'd seen when he was at the station to be interviewed; a Puerto Rican; the playwright whose work Septimus had added a scene to a few nights before; a nationalist from Harlem; and a white professor I'd seen around the Village who was supposed to be some kind of radical. The cat from the PLP seemed to be our leader. He moved to the door and we moved to the door. He crossed Madison and we crossed Madison.

The Cuban Mission to the United Nations was on the block between Madison and Fifth. There were cops all over the place. On the corners. On the sidewalk opposite the building and on the sidewalk in front of the building. Obviously we were expected because the PLP cat just said one magic word to the first cop we came up against and led us all into the block. The cops were expressionless—until you looked into their eyes. I had no trouble imagining what they were thinking: "It's a helluva thing, letting a bunch of niggers, a spic, and a couple of bearded beatniks just walk right in to see their Commie pals. Who knows what the hell they're plotting? I got my orders, but I'd sure like to work those bastards over and then ship them out to Castro, postage free."

"Just touch me," the playwright, a short, fat, black cat, said to a cop, "and I'll have you up for police brutality and giving America a bad name in the UN." The cop stared straight ahead.

"Cool it," said our leader.

"Fuck you, you white mother," the playwright muttered. The cop allowed himself a small smile.

Inside, a young, plump Cuban took our coats and led us into a large room on the first floor. There were couches and a lot of chairs. The furniture was kind of shabby but comfortable. Viera was sprawled on a couch, smoking a cigar and reading the *Times*. Bearded, he was short and compact and gave the impression of having a lot of power in reserve. Physical power. He wore crisply pressed, clean green fatigues. Sitting next to him was the interpreter, a thin cat with glasses. The interpreter wore a black suit, white shirt, and tie. No beard.

Viera gave us each a cigar. I rarely smoke cigars, but man, that one was something else. So smooth and easy. It even smelled good. I wondered if I could ask for seconds.

"We appreciate," our leader said, "you giving us the time to ask you some questions. These are all," he waved at us, "young men who are against American imperialism and exploitation both abroad and in their own country. They are for change and for a redistribution of power in this country."

The interpreter started, but Viera cut him off, nodded, smiled, and opened his arms, like saying, "OK. Let's start." He was a most relaxed cat.

As the conversation went on, it was clear to me that Viera didn't really need an interpreter. Like a few times the interpreter garbled a question—I know some Spanish—and Viera answered the original question, not the interpreter's version. Anyway, it began with the PLP cat asking Viera how it was possible to keep a revolution alive—before it made it and after.

"You have to be a little crazy," Viera answered, "to start a revolution. I mean, if you are realistic and look at the odds against you, it's obvious that only a crazy man would think he had a chance. Then, when you win, you have to stay a little crazy. Of course, you pay for it. We made a lot of mistakes at first. And we're still making them. Running a country is a complicated job. You can't just will into existence bigger crops and administrators who know what they're doing. But if you don't stay a little crazy, you become only bureaucrats. And," Viera smiled, "being as small as we are and as close to you as we are, we also had to stay a little crazy to believe we could survive geography."

John the Avenger said he didn't quite understand what Viera meant by "crazy."

"Crazy open," Viera answered. "Open to all kinds of possibilities, however difficult and remote. Staying creative is one way of saying it. All really creative people are slightly mad. You are a Marxist, you stay a Marxist, but you don't do it by the book. You make your theory creative and you make it flexible because you're dealing with people, large numbers of people, not with books. You have to keep them a little crazy too. Those who have gained from the revolution. The others, the ones who used to be on top or who had a comfortable place and didn't care what else was happening, they're too late to change. But the young are those with whom you build. You have to make work a privilege for them. For them work has to be a reward, an honor to be part of the new Cuba."

"How do you do this?" asked the PLP cat.

"We are trying," said Viera, "in the schools. We are trying by staying a little mad and young ourselves."

"At what point," the white professor broke in, "will you feel that the revolution has been strongly enough established so that there can be other parties and real elections?"

Everybody else in our group looked at the white cat as if

he had a loathsome disease. Viera smiled at him. "You are speaking of the Kingdom of Heaven. We are not there yet."

John the Avenger leaned forward. "What advice can you give us about starting a revolution in this country?"

Viera frowned.

"I mean," said John, "like guerrilla warfare."

Before the interpreter had finished translating John's footnote, Viera barked out a laugh. "*Aqui?*" he shouted. "Oh, no, you cannot make a revolution in the streets here. There is too much against you."

John looked as if he'd found out for the first time that there was no Santa Claus.

"What *can* be done?" the playwright asked.

Viera measured him, and then the rest of us. He leaned back, drew on his cigar. "I am speaking theoretically, you understand." The message I got was that he wasn't really sure whom he *was* speaking to and wasn't going to leave himself open to a charge of using that fine pad, that fine pad for Cuba's Mission to the United Nations, to spread the revolutionary gospel in the host country.

"Speaking theoretically," Viera continued, "and speaking of any large, industrialized, efficiently organized country, there are ways to dislocate without guns. If a revolutionary cadre is itself well organized—and spread out in a number of strategic places—it can create wave upon wave of chaos. If that is what it wants to do, and if it knows how to take advantage of that chaos to get power—first small power, then growing power. There is a direct relationship between how tightly organized a society is and the amount of disruption that can be caused by small but crucial breaks in that system of organization.

"Let me give you a small example. You have huge dairies in which huge numbers of cows are milked electrically. Because of this, there are no longer enough workers in those dairies to milk those cows manually if there were suddenly no electricity. Take the transportation of food. Transportation requires fuel, and fuel comes from fuel pumps, and fuel pumps require electricity. Similarly, it is not too difficult to disrupt an entire city's—and an entire region's—electrical supply. And its water supply. And its gas supply. Factories can be stopped for a sufficient length of time to create chaos in other industries dependent on these factories. And, if you are clever and resourceful, they can be stopped again and again. A sophisticated revolutionary cadre in a large, organized country, for another illustration, should have a core of computer experts who would know how to get at and, let us say, reprogram certain computerized operations.

"But chaos is only the beginning. You have to know where to move from there." He smiled again. "And I am not the right professor for that because I do not know well enough the ways in which power interconnects in—speaking theoretically—this country."

The conversation went on for another thirty or forty minutes, part of it taken up by a boiling speech—not a question—from the Puerto Rican, who was in one of the Puerto Rican independence parties. Viera nodded, agreeing, as that revolutionary talked on, his words whizzing through the room like bullets from a machine gun. But Viera gave him no advice.

Finally Viera looked at his watch, rose and handed out a box of cigars. I grabbed three and I noticed that my comrades did pretty well too. He had, he told us, another appointment. We thanked him, each of us shaking his hand at the door. He was smiling. The good host.

"May your revolution prosper," said John.

"Good fortune to you," said Viera. He patted John on the back and turned back into the room.

Outside we walked past the stiff police. "Try it now," said the playwright to the same cop he'd baited before. "Come on! You've had plenty of practice cracking my kind of head." The cop ignored him.

"Look," said the PLP cat as we got to Madison Avenue, "we'd hardly be repaying Viera for agreeing to see us by creating an incident in front of his place."

"That's how much you know," said the playwright. "You people are pathetic. If we wait for PLP to lead the revolution, we'll all be linked together into one central computer."

"What's *your* strategy?" said the PLP cat, bugged.

"You'll find out, baby. You'll be one of the first to find out."

John chuckled. The two of us got into a cab. "So I'll see you tomorrow," John said right off, obviously not wanting me to give him the recorder and the reels. "Coffee at Riker's?"

"Sure, double-o 7." John glared at me, sunk into his seat, and had nothing to say all the way downtown.

"You got a lot of work ahead of you, baby," I said as I got out of the cab in front of my place.

"That's right!" He sounded for a second like one of the congregation at Malcolm's Muslim meetings years ago. "Work with a purpose. With a goal. What's yours, man?"

"Watching the show. Taking side bets." The cab drove away. Damn, it occurred to me, now I got my picture in some damn FBI file. You can be sure some cat was snapping us on that street. What the hell. They got nothing on me. For some reason, I broke up laughing. They really didn't have.

14

Dianne

A week after he came back to our place, Septimus began to get some carpentry work from Randal's friend. A week after that, he came in one night with a typewriter and a box of paper. From then on, when he wasn't out working, Septimus stayed in that tiny room of his. There'd be long stretches of furious typing, long silences, and then the typing again. He never showed us what he was doing, maybe because neither Billy nor I ever asked him.

One night, after dinner, Billy was fooling with a tape recorder and I was lying on the couch in the living room, reading. I dozed off, and when I was awake again, Billy had gone. He could at least have told me he was splitting and leaving me alone with Septimus. I could have gone over to see Shirley or someone. But Septimus had been so quiet these last weeks, I really wasn't all that worried. A little though. I went into the kitchen to get a paring knife I could put in my skirt pocket, just in case. Septimus must have heard me, because just as I slipped the knife into my pocket, the door of his room opened.

He stood there, a can of beer in his hand.

I looked past him. On the floor beside his bed was a pile of manuscript pages. Hundreds it looked like.

"Crap." He nodded toward the pile. "Too many books being put out anyway. My literary contribution to the world will be not to add one. There are readers who will never know they were spared a few hours of the same old shit about the black boy in the ghetto because I decided never to finish my book. Just think of that. How easy it is to be an anonymous benefactor to who knows how many people." He laughed, if that's what that cold noise was, and went to the refrigerator for another beer.

"Is that what you're doing? *Septimus in the Promised Land? Go Tell It on Top of the Hotel Theresa?*"

"Something like that. More blood than them though. More people dead or chopped up per chapter than in all of Chester Himes's detective stories put together. That's why I know I could sell the book. Average cat gets such a vicarious kick out of ordinary violence. Christ, my book would give him new fantasies to play with for the rest of his life. Maybe I *ought* to get it published. It could save some wives or some kids or some faggots from getting belted. I'm torn between the gifts I can bestow. Silence or vicarious violence. Want a beer?"

I nodded. He seemed quite calm. I sat down at the kitchen table. He leaned against the wall.

"Did Sanders ever sleep with you?"

Septimus could always do that too. Suddenly, out of nowhere, ask you something that made you jump.

"No. He wanted to, but I didn't like him. I was afraid of him."

"I'm glad to hear that. He was the worst son-of-a-bitch I ever knew. Up at Elmira and Coxsackie, we used to trade stories about him. And figure out ways to get him when we got out. Slow, eviscerating ways. You know what one of his

first gigs as a plainclothesman was? Busting black whores.
The way it's supposed to go, the cop comes on like a cus-
tomer. If the girl won't make the first move, he does. Then
he gets her to a room and busts her. But Sanders had his
own style. He'd get them to a room, bang them, sometimes
all night, and *then* bust them. He'd had all he wanted for
free and he'd tell them if they told what he'd done, first of
all, no whore's word would stand up against a cop, and second, when they got out on the street again, he'd find them
and fix them so nobody would take them for free, let alone
pay. It didn't last long. He got too well known, like a walking plague.

"Another thing he specialized in, and this lasted till he got
killed, was being the good soul-brother cop. They'd haul in
some colored cat uptown or in Bedford-Stuyvesant or the
south Bronx and slap him around for a few hours. Then
Sanders would come in and make like he was talking the
white cops out of beating the poor bastard any more. He'd
stay alone with the guy, giving him all kinds of jive. Like,
take a guilty plea and I personally—because I'm tight with
a lot of the assistant DAs—will see you get it light or maybe
suspended. Some in for the first time, some very young,
stupid guys, would bite. Of course, he never talked to no
goddamn DA. Those guys who knew what was going down
would laugh at him or just cool it. I think Sanders liked that
better. That meant he could go to work on them all by himself. I'm convinced he could make anybody talk. There are
things, for instance, that can be done to a man's balls—and
I'm being entirely literal—that would make anybody sell
out his wife or his kid, let alone himself, in under five minutes. He got me once."

"When you were a kid?"

"No, three years after that. I got stopped on the street
with a couple of radios. It was part of the daily haul for

junk. But they really couldn't prove anything. I'd taken them from other junkies who'd taken them from their parents or their sisters or somebody. So nobody was going to call the cops. Nobody does anyway where I used to steal. It's like signing a complaint against the rain. Besides, they know the cops ain't about to go looking for radios. So I was OK. I had those radios for a long time and I was going to pawn them, I said. They knew me though so they took me in. And left me with Sanders. In under thirty seconds I would have confessed to killing Marilyn Monroe after raping her."

"What did he do?"

"Very simple. He didn't lay a hand on me. He knew I knew all about him. From the time I was a kid and from the guys I'd hung around with that he'd sent up. 'Williams,' he said. 'I'm in a hurry. I've got some very tasty pussy waiting for me. And I don't want to get all worn out on you. Listen to me carefully. You talk or I will put out your left eye.'

"That was all. I didn't have the slightest doubt he'd do it. So I talked. I spent a lot of nights after that imagining what I'd do to him one day. Have you any idea what that felt like? Being absolutely powerless. Knowing that bastard could have done anything he wanted with me. I'd often dream I couldn't get up, I couldn't breathe, and then I'd see him sitting on me. That fat, funky ass on my chest and him laughing and laughing like a gargoyle."

Septimus took a long swallow of beer. "I've known a lot of cops," Septimus went on, "and I despise every one of them. But Sanders was one of a kind. Christ, by comparison, he made me feel pretty normal."

"Could—could you really have killed him? I mean not in fantasy. Can you kill, Septimus?"

He didn't say anything for a while. Just looked at me, sipping his beer. "Any man can kill. Some are much quicker to than others. Some can do it only if they're about to be killed themselves. Most never get a chance to kill. And that's too bad. It's one of the great experiences. Partly because it's one of the rarest. Practically anyone can create life. You fuck long enough and you got a baby. But ending a life, that's really putting your mark on the world. A negative mark, to be sure, but one that can't ever be undone. The ending of possibility. That's the closest a man can come to being the all-powerful God. You create a life, you don't know how it's going to turn out. Even if you stick around, you're only one of thousands, millions of influences on that life. You end a life, and you've committed a final act. You've had, for once, or as many times as you do it, the final power. It makes you bigger than life. There's no high like it, if you can let yourself enjoy it."

That's all he said. Nothing about whether he actually did kill Sanders. But the way he said it gave me the chills. And fever. Sick it was, but I was suddenly, unbearably excited. I *knew* he'd murdered Sanders and I wanted desperately to go to bed with him. I was looking at him hard and my mouth was open. He dug. "Want to eat some of the lion's heart?" he said, picked me up, carried me into his room, kicked the door shut, and fucked me. Hard, fast, deep. I screamed, it was so good and full. I cried and I laughed and I almost bit his ear off.

Stretched out, he lit a cigarette for me and one for himself. Then he began to laugh. "If I didn't kill him, you've just conned yourself, baby."

"You've killed before."

"No. I was just running the changes on how it must feel to kill. I've meant to a number of times, but I never quite killed anyone. Before."

"And this time?"

"Baby, I wasn't even in New York that night."

He must be lying, but now I wasn't so sure. I fell asleep and he woke me when he drove inside me again. It was almost as good the second time.

15

Thomas

"I've been through the self-pity bit," Williams was saying, leaning back in his chair, a stiff shot of bourbon beside him. I was watching the level on the tape recorder. I'd decided to handle the taping myself. To hell with Billy and his making out that it would be so difficult for me to interview Williams. It had been going just fine. Randal was sitting across the room, his head against the sofa and his eyes closed, but listening.

"I never had any idea who my father was. My mother died when I was five. I remember the night. It was cold and I was sitting on the floor, gnawing on some cold chicken, and crying for her. Right there I have a psychological out. No father figure and then my mother dies. No chance to resolve the Oedipal cycle. One strike. Black and poor and shunted around to different 'aunts' who really didn't give a damn. And their succession of men who'd beat on the 'aunts' and beat on me. Two strikes. And those fucking schools. Those white teachers and those Jewish principals. 'We made it up from the ghetto but these people are different. They must be inferior. Look at them. They won't learn. They can't learn. Their parents, when they have parents, never show up.' You know that whole bit. So they treated us like animals. And so some of us acted like animals. Three strikes. But, like I said, I'm tired of the self-pity scene. No kicks to it. Not for me.

"When I was a kid, of course, I didn't know enough to have any self-pity. I knew whitey was the enemy but there was no battle going on. So I didn't have much use for most blacks either. They were taking it, the women shuffling off downtown to clean and cook for Mrs. Goldberg and the men going downtown to do the dirty work for Mr. Goldberg. Disgust I felt pretty early, and anger, but not self-pity. Not yet. Besides there were kicks in the street. But you know all that too. And the kicks had to be paid for. I didn't get busted until I was fourteen, in 1946. Sanders. For theft. And then it was stealing a car and later assault and then burglary. I'd get sent away and get out and get sent away again. I had a fairly long stretch on the street in the early fifties. That's when I was a full-fledged member of the junky lodge. I sold the stuff, and I pimped, and I mugged. Considering where I was and who I was, it was a natural scene. What was unnatural was slaving for whitey at some lousy job that left you with no real bread and certainly with no self-respect. At least, as a criminal, I was a free-enterpriser. I had to use my head, and whitey, the cop, was my adversary. I didn't have any damn white straw boss.

"All this time I was reading too. I've been reading ever since I can remember. Damned if I know how *that* addiction started. Curiosity, I suppose, when I was a kid, and then later, it meant I could close myself in from anyone and anything whenever I wanted to. Junk, even when I got good stuff, wasn't ever quite enough. Same with liquor, the times I was off junk. I needed one or the other but I needed reading too. For a time, the reading fucked me up though. I

read enough sociology and popular psychology to start figuring myself a victim. That's when the self-pity poured out.
Poor black boy. Never had no chance. He's what the society
made him. But still, if the poor black boy perseveres, maybe
he can tran-*scend* that *de*-prived background. And that led
to my spending six months in a lousy laundry. Trying to,
like, lift myself *up*. And going to school nights. I was going
to get enough credits for a high school degree. One night *I*
was mugged on the way home from school. They took all
my bread, my books, and even my coat. Christ, I figured, I
must have a badge on me—permanent victim. Fuck that. I
was so goddamned mad, I got rid of the self-pity and went
back into a scene where I wasn't a victim any more. Now I
spent more time on novels, novels that didn't have any neat
theories and statistics about victims. Novels in which victims
and executioners were one and the same, novels in which
love and hate, idealism and terrorism were all screwed up
together. Like Dostoevski, you know. Then a lot of history
and science and existentialism.

"The place I finally found where I was at was a study—a
psychological study—of the people in Hiroshima who had
survived the bombing. The guy found out that what almost
all of them shared was a feeling that death was always
around, that you could bump into him any minute, any second. And that they had no faith left in the structure of existence. I mean nothing held together. There was no fucking
reason to believe in anything. That crystallized my scene. It
was simply absurd to hang on to *any* system of thought.
Nothing ever really got resolved, nothing ever really
changed. There was only death and the beast inside everybody. And the beast certainly had nothing to do with making life any 'higher' than he was. He acted, when he could
get out, only to fulfill himself.

"So I began to contemplate the beast in me. Most of the time I wouldn't let him out simply because I didn't want to go back to prison. But other times, not even the fear of being locked up again could make me a vigilant keeper of the beast. Those were the times when I'd figure, shit, I only got this life. What do I win if I don't let the beast have his way at least *some* times? That was when I did whatever the hell I felt like and to whoever I could get my hands on. If I was angry, I cut and I hit and I kicked. Ever bite off part of a guy's ear? There's quite a lot of satisfaction in that when you're in the mood. And when I wanted sex, I *had* it, for days. With whores, of course, or those close to it. I'd read enough psychology to figure *that* out. The one thing I stopped was junk. I couldn't let the beast out when I was on junk or thinking about junk. Junk was a cop-out high. Junk was a victim's high.

"There was a Chinese general during the Ming dynasty. He set off a huge slaughter, a boss-size slaughter in Szechuan. And what he told the troops was: 'Heaven brings forth innumerable things to support man. Man has not one thing with which to recompense heaven. Kill, kill, kill, kill, kill, kill, kill, kill!' I was with him. The historians call him mad and I'm sure that if anybody in that fucking prison system ever bothered to really apply the conventional psychiatric wisdom to me, I'd be declared a psychopath. At least.

"Words. Mad. Psychopath. Lyndon Johnson isn't a psychopath? And Mao? OK. I do it direct, when I do it. Me and the victim. If the victim was able to let *his* beast out, it might be a fair contest. But most people can't."

"Are you saying, then," I asked him, "that man's nature is inherently and permanently violent—I won't use the value-judgment word 'evil'—and he has never, cannot ever transcend and transform that nature?"

"Now you're trying to get me into systems, into theories again. Look, I finally got to the point where I know that all I know is what *I* know. You tell me man can exorcise the beast and will not ever need him again, will not need substitutes for him, will not need war and cops, and will not need violence all through what he calls his entertainment. And you tell me there won't be husbands breaking wives and wives breaking husbands with violence that may not be physical but is much more vicious and permanent in what it does. You tell me that and I'll believe it when you show it to me. Until then, I'm going to live, part of the time anyway, according to my nature. And my nature requires letting the beast out. I can't let him out all the time because I'd be killed, and another part of my nature is not wanting to die. But I got to let him out some of the time or he'll bite chunks out of me inside."

"Septimus, would you let the beast murder?" Randal asked.

Williams looked at him with a very small smile. "Would I or have I?"

"Either one."

"Yes. And you decide which part of the question I was answering."

Williams got up. "Enough. I'm tired of talking."

I thanked him for his time and held out my hand. He smashed me in the nose. "What the hell—?"

"The beast is hungry," Williams said. And laughed. "You want to give yours a chance to get a bite?"

No, I did not. I wanted him to hell out of there. "Let's go have a drink," said Randal. Thank God Williams agreed and left with Randal. There was blood on the tape. A real authentic documentary. The man was crazy. Billy was right. He could have killed me if I'd interviewed him without anybody else there. I had to talk to Dianne about him. It was nutty, her living in the same house with him. My nose hurt like hell. That son-of-a-bitch. I wished I *could* let out my beast. I'd like to tear him apart. Jesus, that nut could convert you if you listened to him long enough.

16

Randal

We must have hit a half-dozen bars before we stopped at the Cedar on University Place. That cat could drink. It takes a lot to get me stoned, but Septimus still seemed cool when I began to feel really strung out at the Cedar. I could function OK, but I was awfully tired. I switched to beer. Septimus kept pouring down the bourbons. It was too much effort to talk, so I just listened.

"There are times," Septimus was going on, "when I think there can be some meaning to life in a generation or two or three. I read Neill, you know, and Goodman, and maybe if you can start with a kid before he's gotten all fucked up with the greed and the fear and the insularity of adults, you can let him *be* and grow clean and open. Then I figure, shit, it ain't going to happen. Who's going to teach them? I mean where are you going to find teachers hip enough to *let* them be. And then I figure, OK, of course there's nothing you can do to really change anything. OK, but then, if you've still got some desire to make as if you can change something, why not indulge it? Even if you know it's a hype. I mean it's a kick, right? Especially if you can work it out so you can let the beast out and at the same time make a difference in one specific thing by just plain removing it. Something just as bad will probably take its place, but you've done *something*, even if it makes no real difference. I mean you've shown yourself you can do *something*. You can at least change the appearance of the game. The scene, if only on the surface, is different because you've been there. That's not much, but it's *something*. You dig?"

"Either I'm too out of it to follow you or you're drunker than you look. I don't know what the hell you're talking about."

"Look. Suppose I killed Sanders." That woke me up. I looked around, but nobody seemed to be listening. Everybody was yelling into everybody else's ear. Nobody anywhere near us could have heard anything. Septimus was talking low, as he always did. There was nothing to call attention to us. Yet I wouldn't be surprised if Horowitz showed up at my place the next day with a complete transcript. The hell with it. I was too tired to stop him. But still. "Hey, man, cool it."

"I *said* 'suppose.' Look, you remove him. What was he? Forty-five? Forty-six? You save some guys from twenty years of Sanders. They may have to deal with someone just as bad or worse. But in this specific thing, one-to-one, Sanders against *a* man, *a* woman, you've made a difference. You've left an opening, a possibility, not for any change in the system, but for a lessening of the sheer quantity of pain a number of people are going to have with Sanders not around. You follow me?"

I followed him.

"Now, suppose you figured maybe there is a very, very tiny remote chance to change the system itself. You suspend what you know and stretch out for just a second. I mean what the hell? Why not? For kicks. If there is, it's only going to be John the Avenger's way. Dislocate. Chaos. Fuck up the system so it can't work. Kill if it serves to keep the chaos really roaring. Now this obviously requires cats who are ready to take power out of the chaos. That's where I've got no confidence whatever in John and his guys. They're just playing games. But maybe someone will come. A Malcolm with ideas and strategies along with the charisma. Just maybe. I'm just playing, dig? OK. So, somebody like me with nothing else to do can pretend he's helping. Why not? I mean it's like making yourself feel good for a time on juice or junk. We all suck our thumbs one way or another. OK, so how can I help? Killing Sanders wouldn't help. In this context a guy like Sanders you need. Somebody you can hate good, somebody lots of people can hate good. He should have been saved until there are enough recruits for the chaos to start. *Then* he could have been knocked off. But take Horowitz. He's of value to the system. Honest, smart, responsible. Responsible to it, you know? He's in the way of the chaos. You kill him and then you kill any others like him that you find, and that makes sense. I mean while you're letting yourself get high with the possibility that anything makes sense. You dig?"

"Yuh, I suppose I get the idea. You're like preparing the way."

"Right. I'm going to do it. I'm going to eliminate Horowitz."

"Hey, why tell me?"

"I know whites better than blacks. I got that extra perspective on them, being smart and black. You couldn't possibly fink. And I'm tired thinking to myself."

"I appreciate the tribute, but I decline the burden."

"Too late. The thing is how to do it. Best way I can figure is to get him to come after me to bring me in. And then lead him where I can do it fast and quiet."

"OK. How you going to get him to do that?"

"He's been in contact with Dianne. She told me. I tell her enough and scare her enough—I mean really scare her— and she'll call him. And he'll come after me, not just tail me."

"You know, Septimus, you really are a psychopath."

He didn't like that. For six bars he's been calling himself a psychopath, and now I say it, and he looks like he's going to get me before he takes care of Horowitz.

"You got me in the wrong mood, boy. Lay off."

"OK. I retract. I'm going home. My eyes are closing. And I don't want to sleep here."

"Later," he says, and *he* cuts out. I had another stein of beer just to get myself together for the walk home. I began to laugh and had to cover my face. Look at the idiot, giggling all by himself. What broke me up was how cornily symbolic this was. A black psychopath is going to murder an exceedingly rational Jew who works for a system that breeds psychopaths, and me, one of the last of the WASPs, I'm in the middle, absolutely impotent, absolutely out of it. Irrelevant. Superseded in the dray-muh of Our Time. But I didn't feel like laughing for long. I got depressed as hell walking home. There was no question about it. For me to stay loyal to Septimus now was psychopathic. The only decent thing to do was warn Horowitz. And I knew I wouldn't do it. I just wouldn't.

17

Billy

At Riker's I gave John the tape recorder and the reels. All wrapped up in a neat square package inside a brown paper bag. Agent Burnett, in recognition of your services to the Black Nation during the Time of Preparation, you are given the Order of Nat Turner, and your family in perpetuity is hereby made exempt from any future laws concerning the manumission of white slaves.

"Thanks," said John. All of him drooped. His head, his eyes, those long bony arms, his spine. He sat on the stool like a mechanical toy all run down. "Let's walk," he said.

So we walked and walked and finally sat down in Washington Square Park. A cop on a scooter watched us. That brown paper bag. Dumb fuzz. Couldn't tell a wino from a revolutionary. But we weren't loud and he let us alone. On the bench across from us was some white lady with a two-year-old. She scuttled away, dragging the kid after her.

"Welcome to Washington Square Park," I said, "you rapist, child-molester, alcoholic, fuck-sayer, and all-around, all-American black man."

John was slumped on the bench, his hands in his pockets. "Such talk from you, Billy."

"I never said I didn't know what was happening and I never said it didn't bug me. I also never said I expected anything to change."

"I appreciated your taping that, Billy." John didn't rise to the chance to preach. "Actually, I'm going to burn it. Nothing there we didn't know. In general, I mean. He's right though. We hardly know any specifics at all. Where to dislocate. How to stop the machinery. And we sure haven't got a strategically deployed staff. I know nationalists in other cities, you know, but that's about it. I know them and they know me, but we're so far from a plan it's ridiculous."

That was no surprise. I watched the cop riding his coonchaser around the fountain at the center of the Square. Let them hit a couple of white kids, white babies, with that thing, I prayed, and those bastards will be back walking again.

"I left Shirley and the kid this morning."

That's why he was dragging around.

"I got a place uptown. I had to make the break, Billy, not just talk about it. I mean that time is *over,* nationalists with white women, talking race and living different. I mean I had to be straight with myself or just forget the whole thing. I mean we could have made it. I dig her, I really dig her. And the kid. Christ, that's something you can't know anything about, Billy. Having a kid. There's no kick like that. Private kick, you know. And it keeps building. That kid, every time I came in the house, he'd look at me like I was the sun, you know. And he says, he yells, 'Dad-ee!' like those cats in Rome when the Pope comes out. That was his first word. He's nineteen months now, he's got a few others. But the big word with him is 'Dad-ee!' "

"But you can't allow yourself that kind of kick."

"That's right. This is it. I could go on teaching. Probably

do some writing. Have some more kids. Move into a better place. I'd be making it, but just for myself. Billy, we've been fucked as a people. We can only come back as a people. For me to make it on my own is just another betrayal. When I was at Fisk and read *Black Bourgeoisie,* I got disgusted. At my father. He's an assistant principal now. Big fucking deal. At all those people like my father. Making it by themselves and to hell with all the rest left in the ghettos. And later I got disgusted at all the messiahs who aren't living where it's at. Jimmy Baldwin on West End Avenue. Even Malcolm lived in Long Island."

"Isn't this just another con, John? So you move uptown and you feel better, in that sense, but what are you *doing?*"

"That's it. I got to organize. We got a pretty big place. Two apartments next to each other. We're going to pool our bread. I got six guys for sure now and I can get more uptown. I'm looking for young studs. Eighteen. Nineteen. With brains as well as anger. We'll start in with history sessions for them and then for younger kids. And sessions on economics. And meanwhile we'll be building an organization. Block captains and then captains in each house. We'll start, you know, with the things that hurt the most right now. The landlords. The Jew stores on 125th Street. The schools. There are some women up there, Billy, who can raise a lot of hell in those schools if we can get them organized."

"But that's nothing new. Christ, they've got even government bread now for community action programs."

"Come on, Billy. That's all shit. So long as we don't have our own power, government bread is just another way to keep us under control. It's not *our* government. It's protecting itself. Against us. Fuck HARYOU-ACT. We got to get our own thing."

"That's still nothing new. Northern Student Movement is doing that. Other cats are doing that."

"Yeah, but they're not moving people. They're not changing where the power is. That's what we got to develop. Keys to the system. So that people can see how it's all connected and how we can start chipping away at it. And then—I trust you, Billy."

I nodded.

"And then, from some of the people we get, we'll find the right ones. The ones who can learn how to dislocate, who can spread out to other cities and teach special people there. Who can convert special people. Brothers who are getting into places where they can fuck up the machinery."

"You're going to convert the high-rising black bourgeoisie?"

"It can be done, Billy. There was a professor of mathematics in Atlanta who went with the Muslims. I figure he'd have preferred a more realistic scene if it was there. Some of the young ones—the token ones—are getting part way inside. They're getting to know *something* about how it's all connected. You just got to be careful to find out which ones you can reach."

"And then what?" John was as crazy as Septimus.

"That hasn't been figured out yet. But we got time before the chaos. By the time we're ready, we'll know how to make the chaos work for us. And by then we'll be organized, we'll have the swing power to either stop the country or get what we want. Whitey keeps moving out and leaving more and more of the cities to us. It won't be long before Baltimore, Detroit, Cleveland, Saint Louis, will be more than half black. We already got Washington, except we haven't got it because we're not organized. And right now, in more than twenty big cities in the North, we got more than a fifth of the population. And we're breeding, Billy. We're breeding fast."

"John, I'm not going to try to talk you out of anything. If a cat doesn't mess with me, good luck to him whatever he wants to do. But, baby, you're still playing games. You're talking like white folks. You're talking as if all those blacks are the same. As if you can put them all in the same bag. A lot of cats, John, got their little niche. It ain't much. In fact, it stinks. But it's something, and they're holding on. They're not about to let go to start marching behind you. And a lot of other cats are so strung out, one way or another, they ain't going to move for nobody. Like all those cats on welfare. They're not about to do anything to lose *that*. And a lot of others, they're still going after that dream. Be neat, be thrifty, lift yourself, and the white folks are going to let you in. So what have you got, John? Some kids. Some dumb, wild kids. That's some army. You turn your back on them, they'll slice your ass off. The odds against you are so high they're out of sight."

"Like the man said, you've got to be a little crazy. More than a little crazy. There's nothing else I can do. If I stay where I am, with Shirley, with the kid, I'm going to disgust myself so much that I'll be worse for them than not being there. If I stay, I'll turn into shit. I got no choice."

"You taking your gun, John?"

"No, that was for that time, the talking time, the not-doing-anything time. We're not anywhere near where we can defend ourselves that way. If I have a gun now, I'm asking for a bust. And I can't afford a bust now. Later, when we're closer to the time of rebellion, then we'll start collecting guns and other things. When I came to where I finally had to make the break, then I knew I wasn't ready for anything now but planning and studying. And organizing."

"Well, baby, I think you're crazy giving up something you dig for—what?—a vision. A fantasy. But you've got balls."

John still sat slumped. It was going to get worse, I thought. A lot worse. It was like he heard me. "There are going to be a lot of times when I'll want to come back. But I won't. That's why the break has to be clean. I'm not going to see them any more."

"It's none of my business, but what are they going to eat on?"

"Oh, I offered to send what I could when I could. But she's very salty about this scene. She said she'll go back to work and somehow make enough to hire somebody to look after the kid. She'll do it. Shirley's got balls too. And it's better that way. There'll be no connection left. Not even a check in the mail. Much better."

A big black strung-out cat stumbled our way. His pants were stiff with dirt. His shirt too. He had a scraggly beard and there was a cut under one eye that was still raw. He weaved toward the paper bag on the seat between us.

"Give me a taste, man."

"There's nothing to drink in there," said John, opening the bag.

The cat tried to focus on the package inside the bag. It was small, but it could be a pint.

"I need a taste bad, man."

"I told you," said John, "I don't have anything."

The cat grabbed the bag and dug in for the package. John knocked the bag out of his hand.

"You mother-fucker," the cat began to shout. "You turn white or something? I told you I need a taste!"

"Let's split," said John.

The cat stood in front of us. "Look, man," said John, "I'm with you." He went into his pocket and came out with a half a dollar.

"Never mind that shit," the cat threw the money down. "I want a taste."

"Brother, you've got the wrong man. Look, you come up-town, you come see me." John started to write out an address.

"Uptown? Fuck you. Ain't I good enough for down here? Am I making you look bad down here? One thing I can't stand is you mothers who turn white."

"Jesus," said John, and tried to elbow him aside. The cat grabbed for the bag again. John shoved him harder and the cat fell against the bench, sliding on to the ground. Up came the cop on the coon-chaser.

"OK, what's going on?"

John nodded at the cat on the ground. "He wanted a drink but there's no bottle in here." He opened the bag enough so the cop could see the package.

"All right, move along." We moved. And looked back. The cop had the cat propped up on the bench. He talked to him, the cat nodded, or seemed to nod, and the cop rode away.

"Later," said John, staring at the cop. "Like I told you, I can't afford a bust now. I feel like a goddamn Judas, but I can't let this kind of sentimentality fuck me up either. It's too late for that brother. He's a casualty we got to make up for."

We stopped at the arch. I was going east and John was going down to Sixth Avenue to get the A train.

"If it's not a drag," John said, "have Dianne look in on Shirley from time to time. If she needs anything, you can let me know and I can give it to her through Dianne. Here's the address."

"I thought this was going to be a clean break."

"As clean as I can make it. But I'm not beyond what I've been yet. Where I'm going and what I've got to do, I've got to get past where I've been. Next time you see me I'll be further along. But right now, I'd appreciate it if you could see that someone keeps an eye on them."

"OK. I hope you recognize me next time."

"I might, Billy. But I hope not."

I started walking toward Fifth Avenue.

"Hey."

I turned around to John.

"Sanders. I haven't had time to look into it. Anybody know anything?"

"Mr. Sanders, he dead, that's all I know. And that's enough to keep me warm come winter."

"Well, I'm going to look into it once I get settled. I still think it might lead to something."

There went John. He did it. I had to say that for him. He put himself where his mouth was. See you in the papers, John.

18

Dianne

The typing stopped. When he wasn't out doing carpentry, Septimus was having a quiet ball around the apartment—reading, playing records, fucking me when I was
around. I got to like sex with him more and more. He had
such control. He could wait and wait until I was ready—
and at first that took a good long time—and then BANG! I
never realized how cool our neighbors were. God, how I
must have sounded. I never knew I could growl. I never
knew sounds could come from so deep inside me. I never
knew what pleasure was. Pleasure, hell. There are no words
for it. I could *feel* every part of me, every inch of me. Just
thinking about it at work I'd get edgy and could hardly sit
still. And at night, afterward, in the bathroom, I'd look at
myself like I hadn't for a long time. Still the same weight as
I'd been in college. My breasts still firm and small but not
too small. My figure slender but not skinny. My ass small
and high. And that fine soft brown color. Except I began to
wish I was darker. I didn't want to be lighter than Septimus.
Ugh, that Thomas. The thought of his skin, his unfinished
skin, made me sick. I hadn't thought I minded it then, but

thinking about it now, it was like having had a plucked chicken fuck me.

"Ain't nothing like letting go and being an animal," Septimus would say, smoking in bed. "Ain't nothing like letting go. As if sex had rules. As if anything you wanted to do together was dirty. As if being an animal was dirty. Shit, most people miss a hell of a lot of kicks." And we did do just about anything. He took me every which way. From behind, standing up, leaning over, leaning back. Sideways. Frontways. Sometimes it felt like I was suspended in air. He came on like he'd spent time in an acrobatic troupe. One of the things he liked was having me stretch over him, not touching him, supporting myself on my hands. Like a handstand, you know. He'd just lie there and look at me and want me, stretching out the hunger, his penis so stiff. And then, when he couldn't stand it any longer, how he'd fuck me then! And here I'd been thinking all along I didn't care all that much about sex. I liked it now and then, I'd thought, but basically, it was sure over-rated. What I didn't know.

Billy was amused. "If Mamma could see you one night, she'd die of shame. Right there, by the bed, she'd drop dead watching her daughter drop out of the middle class. Drop down, down, down." I sure liked it down there. I never wanted to come up again.

"Septimus," I said one night, "I'm about to believe that thing about blacks being better in bed. Black men and black me too."

He roared. "I'm not that good, baby. I guess you haven't been getting it right. No, that's jive. I've been with some white women, ones who weren't full-time whores, who were really naked and loved it. And here and there I've known white guys I figured got right down to the nitty-gritty any chance they got. Some can let the beast out and some can't."

The beast. He talked about the beast a lot. The beast in bed, reveling in just being, taking. "Sure, I wait for you most of the time, and that's putting a leash on the beast, but I dig hearing *you* moan and growl. Nothing wrong in sophisticating my beast so long as when I let him go, I really let him go." And he also talked about the beast raging, tearing, killing. But I didn't pay that much mind. With me he was the beast having a ball. Until. Until the night he went crazy.

I was stretched over him, aching for him to pull me down. And he reached under the pillow, took out a knife, and sliced at my breast. I was so shocked it didn't hurt at first. I saw the blood and I saw the knife coming again. "I'm going to cut that off," he said, smiling, "to keep with me. To keep in my pocket whenever I want to feel you." I jumped back screaming, shuddering, wanting to throw up. I ran out of the room, screaming, and there was no Billy. I was terrified Septimus would come after me. I must have dressed in five seconds. Running to the front door, I heard him behind me. Naked, his penis still stiff, he just stood there. "I'm gonna get that breast, baby. I got to have that breast."

Thank God there was a cab passing by that late at night. I went to Shirley's. I must have looked like I was coming apart. She didn't ask me anything, just put a robe around me, put me in her bed, got me a glassful of Scotch, sat down, and waited. I couldn't stop shaking. She had to hold the glass up to my lips. I gulped it down. And then another and another and another.

It was still dark when I woke up. Shirley was still sitting in the chair, but she was sleeping. I must have groaned or something because she opened her eyes. She asked me if I wanted anything. I shook my head, got to the bathroom, and threw up. Up and up and up. How could I have had so much in me to throw up?

I was still shaking, but less violently, when I went back to bed. And I could talk. Or pant. I got it all out. I told her the whole thing.

"You stay here until he gets out of there," Shirley said. "I'll call Billy."

"But that's no good. He'll still be *loose*. He'll still get me. He's crazy, Shirley. He's going to cut off my breast."

I remembered Horowitz and told her what he'd said.

"Dianne, it's not being a fink to save your life. Call him. You've got to call him. You're right, that animal can't be allowed to prowl the streets."

The beast. He had told me. I looked down at my breast. It was a small cut. The knife had just penetrated the skin. The blood had dried. I began to shake hard and Shirley brought me more Scotch. I looked at the clock by the bed. It was a quarter of five. I had Shirley bring me my pocket-book. I dug around inside and found the card.

Horowitz sure woke up cool and clear. If he'd been asleep. He listened, and asked for Shirley's address. "Where you are now," he said softly, "will be under surveillance until I get Septimus. Right now though make sure everything's locked. Have you any idea where he'll go?" I didn't. "That's all right. I'll find him. Miss Burnett, I'm terribly sorry you've been subjected to this and I'm very glad you called. We can't let him prowl around loose, can we?"

"No," I shuddered. "No."

"I'll be in touch with you as soon as I bring him in. I can have sleeping pills sent over if you'd like." Yes, I'd like. And that was it. I'd called the keeper and the beast was going back to the zoo.

19

Thomas

That must have been a dream too, the night Sanders was killed. The hammering on the door and my not being able to get up and answer it. Because it happened again a few nights after Septimus and Randal left. I got drunk and fell asleep in my clothes, sprawled on the bed. The banging began, the terrible banging, and again, I couldn't get up. But this time the door broke open. Sanders was in front, his frog face grinning. Behind him were Septimus and Dianne. None of them said a word. Dianne was laughing as she stripped naked and there, right on my rug, goddam it, Sanders humped her. Then Septimus did it while Sanders, smoking a cigar, nodded and grunted encouragement and patted his feet to the rhythm yet. Then she made it with both of them, going down on Sanders while Septimus banged her. They were all laughing, laughing at me. I couldn't move. They were pointing and laughing. Pointing at my erection. And I couldn't move. I was crying with frustration and anger and humiliation. That really broke them up. Sanders slapped his thighs, Septimus doubled up, choking, and Dianne had that put-on smile. She stroked the back of Sanders' neck, moving her lips at me. I could make out "sweetie" but I couldn't hear anything. The sound. The sound. What the hell happened to the sound track?

The phone woke me up. I let it ring, certain they were there, they had been there. But it was just as it had been when I fell asleep. No cigar ashes. The bottle with only a corner left in it. I picked up the phone. It was Billy.

"Hey, is Dianne there?"

I looked at the clock. Jesus, seven in the morning. That was a new one for Billy. The concerned brother.

"No. I wish she were, but she's not. What's up?"

"Nothing, man. She's not here and I just had a feeling. I wanted to find out where she was."

"No, something's wrong. It's not like you to be worried about her. What IS it?"

"Nothing, nothing."

I got scared, scared and angry. "You've GOT to tell me what's happening!"

"I don't got to tell you nothing, man. You're just worrying about your pussy, man. I expect it'll still be there for you." And he hung up.

Billy too. If you're white, you can't be any way right. I remembered my mother saying when I moved out of the house—what was I, eighteen, nineteen?—"Mark my words, you can do business with goyim, but don't be friendly with them. And shicksas, you start in with them, and one day they'll call you a kike. Mark my words." She'd been behind the times. It was black goyim you had to watch out for. You can never make it with them. Sooner or later, it comes through. Contempt. What a mess that would be, marrying Dianne. I must have been out of my skull. Well, fuck them. That was a funny thing to say after that dream. Yeah, yeah, I know. In his subconscious the white man projects all his base desires onto Negroes. My id is Mr. Charlie. How about that? At least in the good old days I could have just taken her and had her as long as I wanted. Yeah, that must have been something. King of the plantation. Take your pick. No wonder those Confederate officers fought so hard. What a deal to lose.

In the afternoon I went into the control room looking for Billy. "Is she all right?"

"Yes. She was staying with Shirley. Sorry I woke you."

"Billy, I'm not seeing her any more."

"Why tell me? I don't care. I'm a liberal."

"I just wanted you to know. I know when I'm not wanted."

"But man, you got to fight for your rights. You got to insist on being judged as an in-di-vid-u-al. You got to picket that girl."

"Lay off, Billy. I've had it."

He laughed. "I thought you Jews had a lot of staying power. Man, you're letting down the race."

I walked out. I wondered what it would be like to work in radio in Vermont. Some town with no minorities but me. And then I'd be the exotic. New York was getting too complicated. You couldn't win. Look at the Jews who'd been in the school system all their lives. That was status thirty, forty years ago. Now they're moved up to be principals and assistant principals. Of what? Stockades bursting with black and Puerto Rican animals. Some status. And politics. The young Jews figure they're with the future in those Reform clubs. The hell they are. I can see them coming to Mayor John the Avenger in ten years. Fifteen years. No room, baby. No room. Our people been waiting a long time and we got a LOT of them to take care of.

I wouldn't mind. They're entitled. If you could work with them. But they don't like us. All right, I know why they don't like us. My mother hated each and every Christian, known or unknown. But how can you work with people if they don't like you? If they despise you? I'm really going to look into Vermont. Where's the new *Broadcasting*? It'll be a while before they spread up there.

20

Randal

Septimus had called in the afternoon. Could I put
him up for a while? OK. I felt a little uneasy, him being as
unpredictable as he is, but except for that moment at the
Cedar, I'd never felt any draft. Personally. And I did like
him. He came over around six with a typewriter and a green
canvas bag. He took out a pile of manuscript, some under-
wear, socks, a couple of shirts, a pair of pants, a sports
jacket, and a toothbrush. There were a half-dozen paper-
backs too. *Last Exit to Brooklyn*, an anthology of Elizabethan
poetry, a Simenon novel, Beckett plays, a Penguin diction-
ary, and some science fiction anthology.

"You travel light."

"Yeah, I took for myself Molnar's advice to Jews. Don't
keep anything more essential than can be put in a bag you
can sling over your shoulder. Certain kinds of roots can
kill you."

He looked beat. "Stretch out, man," I told him. "I don't
go to bed until the morning. Tomorrow we can get a cot."

"No, I can't sleep. I mean I got things to do." He shook
off a drink. "Got to stay clear." He obviously didn't feel like
talking so I started to go through *Down Beat*. I'll be damned

if I know how he got in, but I looked up maybe a half-hour later, and there was Horowitz.

"You're alone?" Septimus didn't seem in the least surprised.

Horowitz nodded.

"I knew I could count on your ego. That's a flaw, Horowitz. You always have to be the big man. I could figure that."

"I'm sorry," Horowitz said, turning slightly to me, but keeping an eye on Septimus, "that this has to be done here. But I couldn't wait. The man is dangerous."

Septimus laughed. "What's the charge?"

"You know. Assault."

I was lost. I thought the bust was going to be for the Sanders murder.

"I'm sorry too," Septimus said to me, starting to get up. "I didn't want to mess up your place, but it had to be done."

Horowitz drew a gun but Septimus' knife was faster. It got him in the gun hand, the gun dropped, and Septimus was on top of him. Just barely because somehow—judo, I suppose—Septimus came flying against the wall, smashed into it, got a chop behind the ear, and just lay there. Horowitz, cool, took out the cuffs, got Septimus' hands behind his back, and locked them.

"This I didn't figure." Septimus' voice was thick. His face had caved in.

"Your flaw," Horowitz picked up the gun and slipped it inside his coat, "is you don't think things through. I'd hardly be unprepared. It is part of my kind of ego to be efficient. And I am a very efficient man. Now, I shall delegate some authority." He went to the phone and called the Charles Street precinct.

"Assault on whom?" I asked Horowitz.

"Dianne Burnett."

I looked at Septimus. It could just as easily have been me. There must be something wrong with me to, like, ask for it. Septimus was staring at Horowitz.

"It's a short rap," Septimus said. "*I'll* be prepared next time."

"No, this one won't be short. If I'd taken you in for that performance of yours at the play, that might have been short. But not this one. I'll make sure you get the right diagnosis this time. I slipped up when I brought you in on that last assault charge. I was less efficient in those days. I knew your record, and even if I hadn't, I could tell. I've had considerable training in abnormal psychology. What I didn't take into account was the idiocy—or perhaps mainly institutional laziness—of the psychiatrists who'd examine you. I'll get you the right one this time. You simply have to be put away, Williams. You're quite hopeless. It's a pity. I am curious, Williams, about one thing. Within the constrictions of your malady, what was the reasoning that made you so eager to get me? You're certainly capable of it, but your attack on Miss Burnett was obviously feigned. Although fortunately the court can't possibly believe that. If you had been serious this time, you wouldn't have let her get away. So why was *I* so urgent a target?"

"Because, you mother, you're in the way of what the future could be like. The way it's going, the guys with the power get fewer and the power gets bigger. For there to be justice, whatever that may turn out to be, it's got to be done all over from the beginning. You were the first step in my career as a demolition man."

"Quite logical. In theory I agree. And I'm rather flattered. But that simply can't happen. We are stuck with and in what we have. We can try to improve it, but we won't get very far. Still one must do something. It is indeed a time for terrorism, even for those without your malady, and I'm sure there will be a rise in terrorism for some years. Isolated, futile terrorism. I'm certainly drawn to the concept. It's noble in its way, that kind of self-sacrifice. Preparing by necessary destruction for a new society, new values. I'm quite taken with it. But it's fantasy nonetheless. It is too late for radical logicians, Williams. Mad or not mad."

"I'll get out, Horowitz."

"You might. I'll try to prevent that by remaining in communication with your custodians. But you might escape. And you might kill me yet. But I can hardly worry about it. After all, I take planes quite often."

Septimus went blank. I couldn't keep it in any more. "What about Sanders?"

"Oh, we unraveled that a couple of days ago. After I'd spoken to you. Detective Sanders received rather primitive justice, but not justice that we can recognize officially. He had a rather new specialty, arresting addicts and small-time pushers. That is, threatening them with arrest and getting paid off for letting them more or less go. For informers on these addicts, he used other addicts, of course. And those he would recompense with heroin, which he coerced, of course, from the addicts on whom he preyed. He cut what he had even more, and once in a while—it could only have been sadism—his bags had only powder and milk sugar. Dummies. This last time he was dealing with an addict-informer in a rather extreme state of need and the addict was not pleased at the deception. Apparently Sanders never expected that a mere junkie could be dangerous for him. He was unprepared."

The cops came and lugged Septimus away, Horowitz following. "I shouldn't worry about your cabaret card," he said at the door. "But just to prevent your having problems with someone else, you might come in and see me. I think I can arrange to get you a legitimate card. You're no danger to the public weal."

I didn't say anything. I certainly wasn't going to thank the son-of-a-bitch.

"You're welcome," said Horowitz. "Ah, the policeman's lot is without love. Or even understanding. But perhaps that's the way it should be to keep what few free spirits are left skeptical of authority. Yes, I should be disturbed if you were grateful."

I got to work loaded. I've had it with juice. I'm going back to pot. Things bug you less with pot.

21

Billy

Septimus writes and writes and writes. Sometimes I answer him, but I don't think it especially matters to him whether I do or not. I mean he hardly ever refers to anything in *my* letters. He just keeps on with what he calls his Anatomy of the New Society. One time it's about the New Education and then the New Economics. He even had a long one about the New Toys. Point one: Ideally a child oughtn't to have any toy he doesn't make himself. Point two: If you let each child follow his curiosity and don't lock him in the same bag as all other kids, he'll be able to make all kinds of things long before he's "supposed" to know how. And like that. A bright cat, Septimus, in his way. But he's out of it. He's really out of it. But I'm saving his letters. You can't tell. Maybe we had a prophet in our midst. The black philosopher. The philosopher of black. Except that he doesn't write about destruction any more. Only about what can come after. Could be a hype. Maybe he's trying to show he's got his beast under control so they'll let him out.

Dianne wrote him a lot at first, but he'd never answer her. So she stopped. For a long time she also stopped going out at night. Thomas would call once in a while, but she fluffed him. Horowitz called a couple of times too. Same thing. Lately though she's begun to have gentlemen callers again. All black gentlemen.

"You're looking for another Septimus, I figure, a fountain that's not cracked."

"Something like that," she said. Mostly she doesn't say much. It's getting creepy here. Too much silence. I may have to find another place. I asked her once why the freeze.

"There's very little to say to you, Billy, because there's very little of you I can reach. Do you still cast a shadow, Billy?"

Shee-it. Free psychoanalysis wherever you go. The hell with her. Who is she? I mean who *is* she? Mamma gave birth to ghosts. Spooks. How about that? Spook spooks. Well, baby, I got my thing. I'm not hung on no job, no place, no body. I get a piece when I want it. I get pot peace when I want that. I'm the free American. One of the few. Living like there's no tomorrow. Because there is no tomorrow. You wake up, and it's today. And if you make your way through today with a minimum of hassles and some kicks, you're making it. That's the only place where reality is at. My reality. Me.

Very few of us free out here. Like Randal. He's making it with his guitar, doesn't get in anybody else's way, stays out of other people's hang-ups. We get different kinds of kicks. Like he's talking about maybe he's ready to get married if he can find someone. OK, maybe it'll work out for him. Sometimes two people can keep each other cool. But whichever way it goes, he knows the score. That's why I dig him. Since I've been the engineer for his jazz program, we've been spending time together. Easy time. He's way past having to be careful about me because I'm black. A real easy cat. I wish him well. Ain't many I wish well. Ain't hardly anyone I wish *anything* about. They're so busy hanging hard to something, about all you can wish—if you gave a damn at all—is that they don't look down. Everybody so damn tense.

They want a really Great Society, they ought to pass out the pot. First President we get who's on pot, first real revolution we'll have. The quiet revolution. Everybody cooling it. Come on, sweet death. In your own time. I'm not waiting for you, and I'm not running from you. Today is it. So simple. If I had a kid, I'd put him on pot early. That's the New Education. Put the kids on pot all over the world, and there's the end of war. Sure, some things got to be fixed. But once you're cool, you can fix them without worrying about what's in it for you. And that means you can fix them.

I was telling that to Randal on the way uptown. He was going to interview an old cat, a guy who'd played trumpet with Fletcher Henderson and Duke and Calloway all those years ago. He was a messenger now, but Randal said he remembered a lot. A lot that wasn't in the books.

"He's bitter," said Randal. "The music has passed him by. No place in jazz for the old. Except a very few."

"That's what I'm talking about. If the guy was cool, if he appreciated what pot can do, he wouldn't waste time being bitter at what can't be changed. Why should he spend his last years hurting?"

"Why don't you give him some of yours, Billy?"

"Well, maybe I will, if he seems the right kind. But I don't know. That's pretty old to start learning something new. Even if it's something good new."

We got out of the subway at Lenox and 125th Street. Halfway up the block, Randal grunted. Like when you put on the light and see a water bug. There was Horowitz, skimming along, a black briefcase under his arm, looking real jaunty.

"Ah," he said, nodding at me and talking to Randal. "How goes the improvising? I've been meaning to come in and hear the new drummer."

"How goes the tracking? Is the scent warm?"

"No, no. I'm not with the police any more. It never really was my métier. Nothing constructive about it. Oh, it was a useful role, but its satisfactions were quite limited. It was all mopping up. You take care of things after the damage is done. The only creativity was in bringing in the miscreant. But you couldn't undo the damage and you couldn't change the miscreant. No, no. I was becoming quite depressed. I had been, as you say, in the same bag too long."

"What are you doing now?"

"I'm with the Office of Economic Opportunity. A scout in the War on Poverty. Sort of a trouble-shooter in the Community Action division. I've had quite a lot of training in sociology, you know. When a Community Action program isn't working out, I come around to find out why. And also, although it's not my primary mandate, to say the least, I try to make sure that there really is participation by the poor. Of course, they can't really *run* things. Then we'd have no money for the program at all. But I do try to work it out so they'll have some sense of participation. It's quite a challenge. Considerably more constructive than, as you put it, tracking."

Horowitz asked us to have a drink with him, but Randal said no, we were in a hurry.

"Goddamn," said Randal, as Horowitz breezed away.

I looked at him.

"Everything gets fouled up. Everything that might give people some hope there'll be a change."

"Why, sure."

"Sometimes I feel like a fink, just playing and not getting into life. I mean just taking care of my own life. You know,

I used to think about going into some kind of work. With kids. Teaching music. Getting up jazz bands for them. There must be some kind of place for me out here. In the daytime."

I let him go on, let him talk it away. He's too hip to really think he's going to change anything that way. But I'm a little worried about him. It's just barely possible that some day he may blow his cool. What a drag. I'd miss him.